ROBERT FORRESTER
THE PIT

Published internationally by Best of Both Worlds, UK

Park Rd, Birmingham, UK

Digitally produced by Best of Both Worlds

For Adrianna & Anderson

ROBERT FORRESTER
THE PIT

ROBERT FORRESTER
THE PIT

In 1970, nearly 300,000 men worked as miners in the UK. Over a thousand deep-pit mines produced coal up and down the country. In Wales, mining was at the heart of many communities with one in ten men of working age employed by collieries.

Today, fewer than 26 pits are open and producing coal, many of these shallow open cast mines. Coal mining employs less than 3,000 miners nationwide.

Some say the mines were closed for political reasons. Some say coal is no longer economically viable. The truth is somewhat more disturbing.

There was another reason they closed the pits...

Chapter 1

When the smoke cleared and Merrick removed his ear defenders, he looked down the freshly blasted tunnel, seeing nothing but blackness.

The darkness felt welcoming to him. An old friend, a work colleague.

'That's opened it up,' Maddox said, as Merrick put the trigger box back in the metal blasting case.

'Let's just hope there's a seam down there,' Llywelyn said.

Merrick stood with Vaughn and Foweather. Like him, they were senior pitmen. Opening up a new tunnel was a dangerous business, too dangerous for regular coalface workers. Merrick was there as ordinance manager, the only man in the pit with access to the blasting shed, the other two were there to check for gas and stress fractures, which could see the entire tunnel collapse around them.

Llywelyn was chairman of South Wales Coal, the company that ran the pit. He was a portly, grey-haired old man whose heavy breathing suggested he wasn't used to the claustrophobic confines of a mine.

Nor was Maddox really, but as senior union rep nothing got done, no decisions made, no new tunnels dug, without his say so.

They stood patiently and held their breaths as the electric lights flickered on at the mouth of the tunnel, slowly revealing a perfectly blasted oval in the rock.

It had taken two months to excavate to this depth. Merrick had spent weeks blasting away the rock, and now it was done. They'd gone as far down as they could go. Everything would hinge on the next few minutes.

His heart pounded with excitement.

The colliery had invested heavily in the operation. Its future, the future of the entire village rested on whether they could find a new seam.

Like most men in Penyrhyll, Merrick was born a miner. His father was a miner. His grandfather was a miner. His great grandfather was a miner. The mine was the heart of the village. Coal was in their blood.

The pit wheel sat in the centre of Penyrhyll like a giant monument. It was the epicentre of their lives, their livelihoods, their way of life.

The winding gear turned continuously, taking men

down as others came up, working 24 hours a day, 7 days a week. At no time were men not down the pit. Merrick had neighbours he had never seen, because when they were on the surface he was down the pit, and when he emerged, they went down.

It was hard, dirty, strenuous work, but it was honest work and it paid well. The union saw to that. And if somebody developed black lung, they would also see to it they received enough compensation to last the rest of their lives, not that was ever long. Few men in the village made it to seventy, and the danger of a collapse or a fire or a damp—the build-up of noxious gasses—was ever present. The plaque in Penyrhyll's church was full of names of those whose lives had been cut short in the pit.

Still, for Merrick and the rest of the men of Penyrhyll, mining was all they knew, all they wanted to know, all they had known for two centuries.

But it was under threat.

They'd been mining the same seam for over a century, slowly cutting through the black rock, leaving pillars of coal to support the great chasm that lay under the village. The pit stretched for miles into the mountains so that below the ground there was nothing but a void. A billion tons of Welsh mountain and countryside sitting above nothing. Because nothing was all that was left.

Or so they feared.

Production had slowed to a record low. Less than a hundred tons a day. The pit was in danger of closing. With it would go the village. Men like Merrick would end up cast onto the great slagheap of unemployment that was beginning to define the decade.

But they weren't going easy.

The Union had brought in some geologists from London. Top men. Graduates from Oxford and Cambridge. If they could find another seam under the valley, the Penyrhyll Colliery might survive, securing the livelihood for 200 men and their families for perhaps another generation.

Or that was the plan.

Merrick and the others looked at each other, knowing how much depended on the next few moments. Foweather checked the gas monitor. He nodded to Merrick and Vaughn, and tentatively, the three of them stepped into the tunnel, the lamps on their helmets casting orbs against the freshly blasted rock.

The tunnel smelled of burned rock and it was hot, oppressively so, almost as if they'd burrowed through the molten centre of the Earth. They were deep. Nearly a thousand yards down. Deeper than Merrick had ever been before in his fifteen years of working for the colliery. Deeper than any mining company in the region had dared to go before.

Yet it looked like it could all be for nothing. The walls appeared to be solid granite, light grey, interspersed with yellow calcite. Vaughn and Foweather swapped shakes of the head. It wasn't looking good.

They strode carefully and slowly, scanning the walls, their feet stumbling on the broken rocks on the ground.

'Careful now, young Dylan,' Foweather said, as Merrick slipped, needing the older man for support.

He smiled an apology and the three men continued into the tunnel, the weak electric lights behind them dying in the blackness until they were alone with only their helmet lamps cutting through the darkness.

'Anything yet?' asked Vaughn, his deep baritone, which made him the prize of the village choir, echoing around the tunnel for several seconds.

'Nothing,' Foweather replied.

'Wait!' Merrick said, his voice breathless with excitement.

His lamp had caught something, a jagged shadow in the erstwhile grey of rock. He stumbled again as he impatiently tried to get closer. This time, neither Foweather nor Vaughn said anything, they too stumbled through the rubble as they hurried to what Merrick's had seen.

It was unmistakable. The dirty black mark in the rock was coal. But it was thin, just a slither. Certainly not enough to justify opening up a new pit, but it could have marked the start of a new face.

Slowly they followed the black line. None of them spoke. With each yard, the seam grew wider. With it, the pounding in Merrick's chest grew more intense.

They were nearly running by the time Merrick's lamp flashed against the end of the tunnel. Here, the seam nearly covered the entire walls of the tunnel. All three men looked at each other, eyes wide with excitement.

They'd found it.

'Mr Maddox, Mr Llywelyn. Quickly!' Foweather shouted back up the tunnel.

They waited for nearly a minute for the hurried footsteps to emerge from the dark.

Llywelyn reached the end of tunnel first and he immediately fell to his knees, his hand pressing against the coal seam. He removed it and examined his palm under his helmet lamp. The all too familiar black mark of coal dust covered his hand. He beamed a smile.

'Looks like your fellows from London knew their business, Owen,' he said. 'I reckon we have a good million ton seam on our hands, boys.'

Owen Maddox, not a man to show much emotion, nodded. 'Guess you'd better tell the board.'

Llywelyn stood, nodding. 'That I will. That I will.'

Then the lights on their helmets flickered out. All of them. At once.

A darkness so black it was devoid of even a single photon of light enveloped them. With it, a cold draft seemed to waft through the hot tunnel, as if somebody had opened a fridge door. Everybody stood motionless, holding their breaths. Then the helmet lamps simultaneously flickered back on again.

'I've told you, we need new equipment,' Maddox said, grumbling and tapping his helmet lamp. 'Now more than ever. If we are to dig this new seam, we can't afford any more cutting corners by management.'

'Hell, you can have sequins on your overalls now that we've found this seam,' Llywelyn said, as they turned and trudged back down the tunnel.

Merrick wasn't convinced. His light and battery pack were new, less than a month old. He glanced over his shoulder back down the tunnel. Darkness had enveloped it again, a darkness that seemed to swirl and dance, a darkness that somehow seemed foreboding, even to a man with coal in his blood.

A chill rippled down his spine. He was going to say something but he knew the mine could play tricks on the senses, and the excitement of finding the new seam was enough to dispel any apprehensions.

So he shrugged to himself and continued with the others out of the tunnel.

Chapter 2

The sound of the brass band, accompanied by the deep baritone of the Penyrhyll Colliery Choir, wafted out of the church hall and across the valleys.

The entire village was in the church hall, many itching for the reverie to stop so they could get to the pub and celebrate the opening of the new pit.

It had been a month since Merrick and the others had discovered the coal seam. And finally, after excavating farther under the mountains, the pit was ready. Extraction would begin. Tomorrow. Merrick would be among the first at the new coalface. Everybody was excited. Everybody was relieved. None more so than Merrick's wife, Emily.

'Do you think we can try now?' she whispered, as Vaughn began his solo, hands clasped proudly before him, head back, booming baritone reverberating.

Merrick nestled his wife's head to his shoulder, the sweet smell of her hair and perfume the perfect accompaniment to the music.

'Perhaps,' he said, gently kissing her on the cheek. He went to stroke her hair, but stopped, not wanting to soil her golden locks with his perennially dirty nails and callused fingers. 'But if we have a boy, I sure as hell don't want him to work down the pit.'

She pulled away, gently, looking at him though wide, doe eyes. 'Dylan Merrick, I thought you loved working down the pit.'

'I do,' he whispered, knowing his words could be construed as sacrilege in the village. 'But it's never going to last, no matter what Maddox says. New seam or no new seam, mining is a dying game, you mark my words.'

'Pah,' she scoffed, nestling back onto his shoulder. 'You've been saying that ever since Thatcher got into Number Ten. You worry too much.'

She glanced around, sheepishly, and then returned her doe eyes on him, whispering gently as she fluttered her eyelashes. 'You know, we could always sneak off after the band has finished and begin trying.'

Her eyebrows gently bobbed up and down and Merrick felt his heart quicken and his groin throb slightly. 'Maddox would notice.'

'Oh, screw Maddox,' she snapped.

'I was hoping it was me that you were going to

screw.'

She punched him in the ribs, and then crossed her arms. 'You just want to get drunk with the rest of them, don't you?'

'C'mon, Em, we've not had much to celebrate these past few months. Let's just let our hair down. We can try tomorrow after my shift.'

'With you stinking of coal dust. Charming.'

Merrick was going to say something, but the music had stopped and following rapturous and enthusiastic applause, Maddox strutted onto the stage, gently clapping the band and choir.

He waited for the applause to die down, before raising his hands, ordering silence.

Everybody obeyed.

The town didn't have a mayor, didn't have a magistrate. They had a single police officer, Constable Eric Barnes, who broke up the drunken fights on a Saturday night, a vicar, Reverend Owen, who looked after the miners' morals, and a GP, Dr Pryce, who looked after their health.

And they had Maddox, who looked after the men's livelihoods and garnered the most respect because of it.

'Thank you, gentlemen,' he said to the band and choir, causing another round of muted applause. He waited for the clapping to stop again, his broad smile in his ruddy, heavyset face twitching a little with impatience.

Finally, he hooked his thumbs into his waistcoat. 'Okay, okay, I'll keep this short. I know many of you will want to get to the Prince of Wales for a pint or two—but those on the first shift tomorrow, take it easy, we don't want any accidents on our first day at the new face.'

A few people laughed, others mumbled and grumbled.

'I just want to say this,' Maddox continued. 'It has been a difficult time for Penyrhyll these last few months, as I'm sure you are all aware, but with this new discovery, I am confident that I can assure you all that Penyrhyll Colliery, which has stood proudly in this valley for nearly two hundred years, will be standing long after we have all gone.'

Cheers erupted from the crowd. Miners, women, children, all clapped and whistled, silenced only when

Maddox patted the air with his hands, as if bouncing two imaginary balls.

'Okay, okay, before you all disappear to the pub or your homes, I thought it might be appropriate if Reverend Owen leads us on a small prayer.'

He waved his hand to the front row, where the Reverend sat. He was an ageing man with whiskers running down his cheeks and a belly protruding over his belt. He stood and cleared his throat, ignored the groans from the younger coalface workers and strode to the front, staring earnestly at his flock.

'Perhaps,' he said, removing his leather-bound pocket Bible, 'you would humour me for a few minutes while I read a little passage that I think is quite appropriate.'

Merrick couldn't see the relevance of the Psalm Owen read out—it was about David's rise to power in the Kingdom of Israel. But then he didn't share in the same religious faith that many of the other villagers did. Sure, he went to church, but he never really believed in it all.

Thankfully, Owen, who was partial to the odd libation himself, kept it brief, and after a booming rendition of the Lord's Prayer and a rousing round of applause, the miners and their families filed out of the church hall and spilled into the Prince of Wales pub.

Chapter 3

Merrick stopped to take a lungful of fresh air before walking through the colliery gates. He employed the same ritual before every shift. It would be ten hours before he would enjoy the clean air again.

He stood and stared up at the Black Mountain. The mountains of the valley dwarfed it, but the Black Mountain was not natural. It consisted of slag—the detritus left over from coal production—piled high into a heap ten stories high.

The giant slagheap cast an ominous shadow over the entire village. Some thought it symbolic of the industry that provided their livelihood. Others feared it. In 1966, a slag pile of a similar size collapsed and slid onto the village of Aberfan, burying among other buildings the local school. Over a hundred children were killed instantly. All mining communities mourned the tragedy, but despite persistent promises by the National Coal Board to remove the heaps, nearly every village where mining took place had their own Black Mountain.

Merrick didn't dwell on it. Today was a fresh start

for the entire village, so he strode through the colliery gates whistling, glancing up at the spinning flywheel that loomed over the pit before heading change and clock-in with the other workers.

In the locker room, Merrick found a clean, brand-new set of overalls and boots, which he placed back in his locker for the time being, knowing that they'd take a week at least to wear in, and a new helmet.

As he readied himself, he chatted to the other men honoured with being the first down the new pit. Everybody was excited. They dressed in quick time, donning their orange overalls, before heading to the lamp room.

The lamp room foreman was an old pitman by the name of Conner. He'd served forty years in the mine but now spent his days behind the lamp room desk, the skin of his broad, flat face the texture of an ageing leather sofa, his breath raspy from decades of coal dust as he muttered the same words to every miner.

'Where's ya token?'

All coalface workers were issued three unique tokens. One was kept by Conner, another handed to the elevator foreman, and the third, the miner kept on him at all times. The tokens made sure everybody knew who was down the mine at any given time. It was a system that evolved two hundred years earlier and hadn't changed much other than the old brass tokens being replaced by chits of plastic.

After Merrick handed over his token, got his lamp and battery and affixed them to his helmet and belt, he waited with the others.

All eyes were on Jerome Reese, the shop steward, who stood by the door leading to the pit wheel, finger on his watch.

Reese was Maddox's right-hand man, a union shop steward. Most of the men didn't like him, seeing him as a bit of a sneak, but Merrick and Reese went back a long way, since school, and Reese's wife, Mary, was good friends with Emily. Mary had not long had a baby, a little girl called Catherine. Merrick suspected this had urged Emily into wanting to start a family of her own.

Only when the exact second passed, did Reese sound the hooter by thumping the button behind him, signalling the official start of their shift.

He then opened the door and they all filed out

after him to the elevator under the pit wheel. Reese pulled open the metal gate and let each man in taking their second token as they filed past.

The elevator held fifty men, all cramped into a metal cage turned black by decades of coal dust. Below their feet, the shaft dropped nearly 1000 yards, and all that prevented the elevator plummeting to the ground was the metal cable connected to the pit wheel and attached to a second elevator at the bottom of the pit. As one went up, the other went down.

Even after fifteen years of working down the pit, Merrick felt a flutter in his stomach as Reese closed the door to a clang of metal.

The chatter increased as the excitement and trepidation grew. None of them had ever worked so deep before. Only Merrick, Foweather and Vaughn had been down to the new face. Foweather was scheduled for the next shift, but Vaughn was there, standing with Reese at the elevator controls. For the rest, it was something new, something to boast about, to go nearly a kilometre below the earth. A record for any pitman in South Wales.

After a jolt, and the whirr of the pit wheel, the

elevator descended. It would take nearly twenty-five minutes to descend, passing rock faces and abandoned pits like the floors of a department store.

The excited chatter quieted with each yard they dropped. The temperature changed too. First getting cooler, forcing the men to turn up their collars and cross their arms. Then it warmed, turning the cramped metal cage into a sauna as drafts of hot air wafted up through the metal grate of the elevator.

Merrick remembered one of the company men telling him once that when you hit fifty feet, the temperature below the earth increased by one degree every ten feet you went down. He tried to calculate how hot that would make the coalface, but maths was not his strong point.

A little after ten minutes into the descent and the ascending elevator flashed passed. Halfway. Normally, it would have been full of men finishing their shift. Today he knew it was empty. No men had been working in the pit. Merrick and the men surrounding him were the first to dig the new coalface.

When the lift finally jolted to a stop, Reese, who

acted as ventilation officer, declared they'd hit a hundred and ten degrees Fahrenheit, causing an array of gasps from the miners.

'That's hotter than when me and the missus went to Greece,' said Vaughn. He was an older hand, grizzled face, tattoos running up his arm. A few others complained loudly, asking Reese whether it was against union rules to allow them to work in such heat.

'We've agreed with the management that you'll all get a five-minute water break at the top of the hour,' he explained. 'Keep yourselves refreshed, lads, and you'll do just fine.'

'Easy for him to say,' Vaughn whispered, as Reese opened the gate and checked the ventilation and gas readings. 'Standing by the ventilation shaft taking readings ain't exactly hot work, is it? With no coal train running, we'll be used up by the time we get to the face.'

'We'll cope,' Merrick said. 'Besides, it's Colliery Board's time we're wasting. I don't mind earning my money walking to and fro.'

'Yeah, but how we meant to get the slack to the

surface?'

Merrick shrugged. 'I think the plan is, we just open up the seam, pile it up, and when the coal train's up and running, we'll spend a few days loading it up.'

After checking his readings, Reese gave the all clear. 'All right, lads. None of you is new to this, so single file, lights on the man in front. No stopping. Dylan, you been here before so lead the way.'

Merrick nodded.

'After you, son,' Vaughn said. 'C'mon, clocks a ticking.'

Merrick stepped out into the tunnel and glanced down the long, dark tunnel, and felt something he had never felt down the pit before. Fear.

Chapter 4

Richard Davies trudged after the other miners ensuring to keep within an arm's length of the man in front. He stomped through the gloom reluctantly. His head ached, having spent the entire night drinking in the Prince of Wales, and he felt nauseated, not having had the stomach for breakfast.

The electric lights were strung every twenty yards so that they walked from gloom to bright to gloom to bright again. The changing light did little to ease his hangover. Every ten yards, iron girders supporting the craggy walls and roof flashed by, breaking up the monotony of rock, but Davies kept his eyes focussed on the ground where rubble and shale waited to trip him and sprain an ankle.

They had been walking for at least an hour and he was exhausted, and he still had a six-hour shift of heavy, backbreaking work to look forward to.

He hated it.

He'd been a miner since leaving school the previous year. Having been brought up in Penyrhyll, there was nothing else he could do. His father was a miner, his older brother Thomas, who tramped just ahead of him, had been down the pits since he was fifteen.

Davies had known from an early age what his destiny was. They all did in Penyrhyll. You went to school, you grew up, you went down the pit. But he longed for something else. Anything.

He wanted a job where he didn't come home every night covered head to toe in coal dust. A job where he could keep his fingernails clean. A job where he didn't have to sweat and labour in the gloom. A job where he could feel the sun on his face occasionally.

He imagined what it would be like to work in a clean shirt, in a cool, air-conditioned office, flirting with the typing pool, going to meetings. But there were no office jobs in Penyrhyll. No offices. Just a few shops and a pub, and they wouldn't pay the same wages as the colliery did.

Even as a junior pitman, Davies took home three times the money than his sister who worked at the grocers. He got fifty pounds a day in danger money alone, not to mention the seventy-five pounds shift money on top of that. He earned more money than he knew what to do with, but he'd trade it all to work somewhere, anywhere, other than the pit.

It was hot, swelteringly so. Sweat poured off his brow and soaked his shirt under the arms. He paused to take a swig from his water container. All the men carried one. They held two gallons but it would all be gone by the end of the shift. He guzzled greedily, knowing the cool water would eventually turn warm in such stifling conditions.

Sensing Davies slowing, his brother Thomas turned round, his head lamp flashing across Davies' eyes. 'Keep up, and what you drinking for? We ain't even started our shift yet. You'll have nothing left for when you need it.'

Davies ignored him, the way younger brothers always ignored their older siblings. Thomas was not like him. He loved the pit. Was proud to be a miner. So he couldn't understand why his younger brother didn't share the same enthusiasm. During their shifts, he would be forever railing at Davies for not working hard enough, for taking too many breaks, for not pulling his weight. It simply never occurred to him that his younger brother hated the job.

But what could he do, thought Davies, as he screwed the cap back on his water drum. His destiny was written long before he was conceived. He was born a miner. He would die a miner.

As he slung the heavy water drum back on his back, something flashed by in his peripheral vision. A shadow.

At first, he thought nothing of it. The way the electric lights were interspersed through the mine often made the shadows dance, so he continued to shuffle after the others.

Then the shadow flashed by.

He stopped, glanced around, but saw nothing in the gloom.

'Will you keep up,' Thomas hissed, turning around.

Davies trotted after him, head shaking unsure if it was his hangover or the lighting that was playing tricks on him.

Then something brushed past him. It was the gentlest of touches, just enough to excite the hairs on the back of his neck and send a cold chill trickling down his spine.

He stopped, turned, saw nothing, and then turned

back again.

And found himself alone.

His brother, who'd been a couple of yards ahead of him, had disappeared. The fifty miners tramping through the mine ahead of him had gone too. Vanished. All of them.

The empty tunnel was silent other than the humming of the electric lights and the thumping in Davies' chest.

He shouted for his brother.

'Thomas! Thomas, where the hell are you all? This ain't funny.'

Then the lights in the distance started turning off, the sound of the relays clicking as each one failed. One by one, from both directions.

Click.

Click.

Click.

The darkness raced towards him from both sides, closing in like two black tidal waves, surrounding him in a sea of darkness.

He'd experienced a blackout before. They all had. It was part of their training. Darkness didn't do it justice. Most people had experienced darkness, but Davies knew only miners and those born without sight knew the totality of a world devoid of all light. It was oppressive, suffocating, all consuming.

He screamed and pressed his back against the wall, remembering his training. During a power outage it was so disorientating, you could walk in circles and have no hope of ever finding your way out. At least with your back to a wall, you could follow the cold touch of the rock.

His breathing turned rapid as the darkness continued closing.

Click.

Click.

Click.

Eventually, all the lights in the mine had gone out, except the one behind his head.

Then. Click.

Feeling the rock pressing into his back, he could hear his breath panting from him, but he could hear something else too.

Whispers.

He whimpered as the sounds washed around him.

Voices. Not male, nor female, not children. He couldn't make out words, yet they sounded like they were taunting him, their hushed tones accompanied by a cold breath that licked at his skin, puckering it.

He screamed, terrified, and called for his brother, called for Mr Reese and Mr Merrick and Mr Vaughan and Mr Maddox and every name that came to mind.

And when the whispers became even more taunting even more cruel, even more merciless, and the cold breath snapped at him like invisible pincers, pinching, stabbing, tearing the flesh on his face and neck, he called for his mother.

Then the blackness washed over his face and smothered him like the press of a cold pillow and his senses disappeared into the darkness.

Chapter 5

They'd just started chipping at the rock face when Thomas Davies scampered up to Merrick, his face already black from coal dust.

'Mr Merrick, I can't find my brother.'

Merrick was at the scrubber, the big cylindrical drum that broke up rock. It was new, the maker's stickers still covering the control panel, but it was different to the last one he had used and he was trying to figure out what all the dials and knobs did.

'What do you mean?'

'Richard, he isn't here?'

Merrick frowned at the scrubber, the controls unfathomable to him. 'Was he on shift?'

'Yes, we came down together but I can't find him now.'

Merrick glanced about. The Davies kid was familiar to him. Merrick had twice had to give him a warning—once, for finding him by a mine cart, sleeping off a hangover. He waved his hand to Reese over by the ventilator, the cool breeze ruffling the shop steward's overalls.

'What is it, Dylan?' Reese asked, strutting over.

Merrick glanced over at Thomas. 'Richard Davies.'

Reese sighed and glanced left, right, as if looking for him. 'What's he done now?'

'Can't find him,' Thomas said.

'Is he on shift?'

'Aye, he was with me, but when we set up, I looked around for him but he ain't about.'

'Maybe he turned back. Finally decided to hand in his cards,' Merrick said.

'When did you last see him?' Reese asked.

Thomas shrugged. 'He was behind me not more than ten minutes ago, but I haven't seen him since we got to the face.'

Merrick gave Reese a look, a look that said no matter what the union said, if the kid was shirking again, he was for the high jump.

'Somebody best go look for him,' Reese said. 'This tunnel is still new so there was a lot of rubble on the way up. He might have tripped, banged his head.'

'He might,' Merrick said, unconvinced.

'Who's on medical?' Reese asked.

Merrick squinted his eyes as he recalled the day's

shift roster. 'Boyce.'

He waved him over.

Boyce was a tough-looking brute with hands the size of shovels. Nobody feigned injury when Bevan approached. It was like being tended by a bear.

He spat coal dust from the side of his mouth. 'What is it?'

Merrick nodded to Thomas. 'Davies' brother. Gone AWOL. Again.'

Boyce rolled his eyes as Merrick jabbed his finger at Thomas. 'You come with us, but I tell you now, if that brother of yours is taking the piss, he's gone, d'ya hear?'

Thomas nodded and all three set off back down the shaft.

Chapter 6

Llywelyn scrubbed at his forehead as if trying to iron the wrinkles flat. 'What do you mean, gone?'

Merrick and Reese shook their heads in unison. 'Gone. No sign of him.'

'What about his tokens?' Llywelyn asked, the narrowing of his eyes creating more wrinkles.

'Shaft token is here.' Reese dropped the small plastic disc on Llywelyn's desk. 'His lamp chit's still in the lamp room.'

'He went down and didn't come up,' Merrick added.

Llywelyn shrugged. 'Then he must still be down there somewhere, had an accident or something.'

Merrick shook his head. 'We've been up and down that tunnel three times now. Even if he was trying not to be found, there's nowhere for him to hide. That shaft is new—there ain't any rooms cut in the rock, there ain't even any slag heaps. Nothing.'

'Well, he can't just have vanished into thin air,' Llywelyn insisted.

Reese and Merrick glanced at each other, the

whites of their eyes standing out amid the coal dust covering their faces.

'That's exactly what we're saying,' Reese said.

'He ain't in the pit,' Merrick said. 'I'm sure of that, and he didn't come up in the lift.'

Llywelyn shook his head. 'Then he obviously never went down in the first place. Must have handed his shaft chit in and shirked off. Wouldn't be the first time somebody has tried that.'

Reese looked down at the token on Llywelyn's desk, his head shaking. 'His brother swears he came down with him.'

'Then he's lying, covering for him.'

It was Merrick's turn to shake his head. 'Not Thomas. He's a good pitman. I know they're brothers, but he knows the severity of something like this. He wouldn't risk his job, not even for his brother.'

'Then he must still be down there,' Llywelyn insisted, shaking his head. He then looked hard at Reese, his eyes turning to large orbs. 'Maddox doesn't know yet, does he?'

'Not yet, but I have to report it.'

Llywelyn appealed to Merrick, his eyes bulging.

'Get back down there and go find him. Take as many men from the face as you need—shut the whole damned mine if you have to. I want him found. If Maddox takes this to the union, we'll have another bloody strike on our hands. Worse, the coal board might shut us down. You know the safety record here hasn't been great. For your jobs, gentlemen, go bloody find him.'

Chapter 7

Mary Davies was bereft. She cried uncontrollably, as Thomas, her son, his hands still black from coal dust consoled her with an arm around the shoulder. The woman had already lost her husband to the mine. His oxygen canister still sat in the corner of the room, serving as a mawkish memento of the months leading up to his death.

Merrick, Reese, Maddox and Llywelyn stood in her cramped sitting room, a quaint parlour decorated in flock wallpaper complete with ornate ducks flying up the wall and the ubiquitous Green Lady print.

None of them had answers for her questions.

'What do you mean disappeared? Where has he gone?' she asked, in between sobbing induced spasms.

Maddox and Reese swapped glances with each other.

'I'm afraid we do not know,' Maddox said. 'I still hold out hope that we find him alive and well, but it's been eighteen hours now, and we've searched every shaft in the pit, and there is no sign of him.'

'But he can't just have vanished,' she cried. 'He

must be lying injured somewhere. You must keep on looking.'

'We will,' Llywelyn promised. 'And I've ordered a thorough investigation, and Mr Maddox is right, there is still hope we will find him alive and well.'

Merrick shifted uncomfortably. Work had stopped at the coalface. Every pitman in the village had been seconded into the search, but Maddox was right. He wasn't in the mine. They'd searched every shaft, every nook, every cranny. They had even scoured the village, checking the pub, the river where Richard and his brother fished, but there was no sign of him.

It was a mystery. There was no way he could have got out of the mine, not without his token, and if he had suffered some accident, they would have found him by now. The pit was new, the shaft a single tunnel, admittedly it stretched for three miles underground, but there was nowhere for him to hide.

There were no tunnels, no offshoot rooms, no cracks large enough to conceal a man, and all the other coalfaces had been sealed off. The elevator had not stopped anywhere other than the new pit, so there was simply no other place he could be.

He had definitely clocked in that morning, and Thomas was adamant he was with him when they descended in the elevator, and Merrick did not doubt his word. Thomas was not the sort to cover for his brother.

It was as if he had vanished into thin air.

'Don't worry,' Llywelyn said patting Mrs Davies' knee as she shook with weeps and sobs. 'We'll find him.'

Chapter 8

In the five months since Davies disappeared, life had changed for Merrick. Emily was pregnant. The pair were expecting their first child in four months' time, and things were looking good.

The new mine was proving more fruitful than anybody at the colliery had imagined. With bonuses and overtime, Merrick was earning more money than he had in all his time as a miner.

He still thought about Davies each morning, stopping under the shadow of the Black Mountain and staring at the pit wheel while wondering what had happened.

They had buried an empty casket, held a service attended by the whole village, yet nobody had any inkling as to what had happened to the young miner.

Merrick had heard all sorts of theories: he had tried to sneak out to avoid his shift, falling down the elevator shaft, even though Merrick had personally checked it; he'd fallen into a sinkhole that had since been covered up by seismic activity, despite the new tunnels being comprised of solid granite; sick of mining, he'd run off to Cardiff to find work in the city with his sister, even though she was at the funeral, her tears as genuine as her mother's.

The truth was, nobody knew, but as with every catastrophe that had befallen the mine in the past, people pushed it to the back of their minds, and life went on. Especially with the new pit being so bountiful.

Merrick found the work hard though, even with his experience. The added distance to the new face meant his shifts rarely lasted less than twelve hours, and he couldn't get used to the heat. None of them could.

'Anybody got any spare water?' he asked, as he sat slumped with Vaughn and some of the other pitmen during their afternoon break, faces covered in coal dust, overalls tied to their waist, bare chests exposed and just as black.

'No, I'm out,' Vaughn said, shouting above the din of drills and machinery and men shouting. He shook his water drum. Sweat dripped from his nose like a leaking tap. 'They need to get a water pipe installed down here.'

'Why not ask Maddox, that's what we pay our dues

for,' Foweather said, pointing to the shop steward standing at the ventilation shaft.

He'd taken to spending the odd shift overseeing safety. Merrick knew the man was worried. The National Coal Board as well as the Health and Safety Executive had carried out inquiries since Davies' disappearance. Neither had made any conclusions but it meant the Penyrhyll Colliery was under scrutiny.

Maddox noticed the men looking at him and he strutted over, finger jabbing in their direction. 'Put those damned overalls on properly—do you want this pit to close down?' he shouted above the cacophony of men drilling.

'It's too hot, Owen, we cannot work in these conditions,' Foweather complained, his voice barely audible above the din. 'You need to speak to Llywelyn, get him to install a drinking pipe down here.'

'Have you any idea how much that would cost?' Maddox said. 'You've got your drums.'

'They're empty,' Vaughn shouted, the light on his helmet wobbling across Maddox's face as he shook his head. 'We cannot carry enough to keep us going. You are meant to be looking out for our welfare.'

'I'm meant to looking out for your livelihoods,' Maddox snapped. 'You know the situation. This Tory government is looking for any excuse to close the pits. We stop being profitable, or we have any more ... incidents, and you can kiss goodbye to your jobs.'

'So, are we meant to die of thirst?' Vaughn said, tipping up his empty water container.

Maddox fumed for a moment, before pointing to the mine train behind the scrubbers that had carried them all to the face. With the Davies incident, its installation had been delayed by over a month, meaning they had to walk the three miles to the face for weeks before it was up and running, leaving them exhausted. Even with the train now running, the oppressive heat meant they were still exhausted by the end of their shift when they would slump into its dirty carriages.

'I've a drum with my snack box,' he shouted. 'You can have that.'

Vaughn staggered to his feet and shuffled off towards the mine train, avoiding the working miners as they scurried around loading carts and conveyors, operating drills and other machinery in a melee that would have been confusing to anybody other than a pitman.

'Do you really think the Tories want to close the pits?' Foweather asked above the noise.

'Of course they do,' Maddox said. 'If we can't get Michael Foot into Number Ten at the next election, the coal industry will be dead in Britain, you mark my words.'

Merrick felt like saying something but thought better of it. Being a miner, it was assumed everybody in Penyrhyll supported Labour. While Merrick was hardly political, he couldn't help but admire the new government. Thatcher, loathed by everybody else, had at least introduced the policy of allowing council tenants to buy their homes. With a baby on the way, even he and Emily had discussed the idea. A homeowner. That was something he never envisioned he'd ever be. Yet he'd dare not voice such a thing down the pit or anywhere else in the village. To have Tory sympathies was akin to devil worship. Besides, his throat was too dry and the noise too loud.

'Where's Vaughn with that water?' he said, craning his neck and squinting at the train down the shaft, trying to see if any of the helmet lamps dancing in the gloom belonged to Vaughn.

Foweather got to his feet. 'He better not be guzzling it all himself.'

'He wouldn't do that,' Merrick said, also standing.

'Then, where the hell is he?' Vaughn said.

Merrick shrugged. 'I'll go see.'

He trudged down the narrow gauge rail line to the miniaturized train sitting just beyond where all the men worked. It would not have looked out of place at a fairground, but despite its small size, it was able to transport fifty men to the coalface and transport a hundred tons of coal to the shaft elevator, running up and down the line at least five times a shift.

The carts were nearly full, coal sitting high, but Maddox stored his gear in the diesel locomotive at the front, a privilege for being a senior shop steward. The men had to make do with a quiet corner where their snack boxes and flasks and water drums got caked in coal dust.

Merrick saw no sign of Vaughn. Confused, he glanced behind, positive he must have walked past him. It was easily done. After a few hours in the pit, everybody looked the same, black faces and black overalls and even in well-illuminated areas like the coalface, you counted lights, not bodies, but Merrick couldn't see any lights nearby.

He reached into the loco. Maddox's water drum sat with his sandwich box below the passenger seat.

Merrick frowned, looked down the line at the rest of the carriages, and saw nothing but the endless black tunnel that ran all the way to the elevator shaft. It was dim, the lights only spaced every twenty paces or so, but there was no tell-tale helmet lamp bobbing in the distance.

So where had he gone?

His foot caught on the ground. He crouched, picking up a helmet complete with the umbilical-like wiring attaching the battery pack to the lamp, which was on.

A cold chill replaced the stifling heat. It trickled down his spine as if somebody had poured ice-cold water down his back. His heart quickened, and he glanced about, like a parent losing sight of a toddler in a supermarket.

A terrible realization dawned on him and he raced

back to Maddox, waving the helmet.

The Union man's eyes narrowed as they caught sight of him, and widened further as he saw what Merrick clutched.

Nobody spoke. Maddox just grabbed the helmet and checked the number on the lamp with his register, a filthy creased piece of paper on a clipboard by the ventilation shaft.

Foweather looked at Merrick who looked at Maddox. All three looked back down to the train and back to one another.

'Tell the men to down tools,' Maddox said, or his lips did. If he spoke, Merrick never heard the words but he didn't hesitate and cantered over to the siren hanging on a bracket, blasting it into the dust-filled air.

Slowly, the sound of drills and machines and men's voices ceased, and the mine fell silent and everybody stood and stared, aware something was wrong.

Chapter 9

'And you've looked for him?' Llywelyn asked, his face stretched taut with anxiety. He looked like a man on the edge: hair awry, as if he'd been pulling at it, tie halfway down his shirt, wells of sweat under his arm, despite the fan on his desk wafting cool air around the office.

'Of course. We scoured the line all the way back to the shaft. He's nowhere,' Maddox said.

Llywelyn's face twitched. 'But you've not done a proper search of the coalface?'

'I thought it best we get the men out,' Maddox said. 'I'm not risking anymore lives until we know what's going on.'

Llywelyn, normally a quiet, fawn of a man, pounced to his feet, slamming his hands onto his desk. 'You'll bloody well do as I ask, if you know what's good for you! If Vaughn's dead, you know what that means, don't you? This colliery is finished, and before you start pontificating and slapping your chest at me, Owen Maddox, bear this in mind. Without this mine, we are all on the scrap heap, all of us.'

His eyes fell on Merrick, who stood with Foweather, heads bowed, confused as to what was going on. First Davies, now Vaughn. Sure, Merrick could understand Davies getting into trouble. He was young, fickle, averse to hard work, but Vaughn was a pitman to his core, you cut him he'd have bled coal. Merrick could not understand what possibly could have happened to him.

Neither did Llywelyn, Merrick judged by the way he appealed to him with doe eyes. 'You're a good company man, Dylan. I want you to take ten men, get down there, look for him. He can't just have bloody vanished.'

'Why not?' Maddox said. 'Davies did. We've got problems, Mr Llywelyn, and until we have sorted them, I forbid any more of my men from going down that pit.'

'Your men!' Saliva spurted out of Llywelyn's mouth as he spoke. 'They're my men! I pay their wages, not you. If you are so bloody concerned about their welfare, you go down the pit and look for Vaughn. Take Reese and the other shop stewards—it's about time you made yourselves useful.'

'I'll go,' Foweather said, helmet clutched in his hand.

Llywelyn and Maddox were too busy casting daggers at each other with their eyes to hear, so Foweather repeated himself.

'I'll go!'

Maddox and Llywelyn glanced at him.

'You'll do no such thing,' Maddox said, his face flushed red.

Foweather looked at him with one eye open, the other half closed. 'You can't stop me.'

'You see if I can't,' Maddox snapped. 'If you go down there I'll...'

'You'll what? Mark my card? Kick me out the union? Without this pit, I'll no longer be a miner anyway, so what's it matter. No, I'm going. I'll take some of the older hands. We'll find Davy Vaughn. Me and him go back far too long to leave him down there.'

'You're not going without me,' Merrick said.

Foweather placed a filthy hand on Merrick's overalls. 'You've a young 'un on the way. You stay. Look after that pretty wife of yours. Let me and the older heads deal with this.'

Merrick protested, but Foweather had a mean look in his eye, like a soldier needing to avenge his comrade. Merrick knew the man was stubborn when he wanted to be. Besides, if Merrick was honest with himself, he didn't want to go. For the first time in fifteen years, ever since he first donned a helmet and lamp and ventured into a pit, he felt scared. Something wasn't right. Men didn't just disappear. They had accidents, yes. They died, all too frequently, but they never just vanished.

Maddox's face twitched and jerked while his cheeks flushed redder and redder, but if he was after a fight, Foweather was the wrong man to challenge.

Eventually, his face softened and he nodded. 'Okay, take ten men with you. No more. Experienced men. Make sure you take fresh lamps and batteries. Water too, and the first sign of trouble, you come back up, d'ya hear?'

Foweather nodded solemnly, glanced at Merrick and strode out.

And that was the last Merrick saw of him.

Chapter 10

Merrick had stood vigil with most the other villagers under the shadow of the Black Mountain all night, eyes fixed on the pit wheel.

Hour after hour passed, but nobody emerged.

Nobody could understand it. Losing Davies had been unfortunate, Vaughn unfathomable. Losing the eleven most experienced miners in Penyrhyll was something else.

People were scared, and did what God-fearing people did all over the world when they got scared, they went to church.

It offered Merrick no solace. He'd never been a believer, but like his politics, his atheism was something he kept to himself, and the next morning, Emily clutching his arm, he strode into Penyrhyll Presbyterian Church with all the other villagers.

Maddox was there and Reese and all the other pitmen of the village, along with old Dr Pryce, Eric Barnes, the local constable, as well as the wives of all the men and their children. All crammed into the tiny church so that more people stood than sat on the burgeoning pews, the aisles four deep.

The only face not present was Llywelyn's. He was still trying to figure out what had happened, no doubt, but even if he had turned up, Merrick reckoned he'd have been lynched.

The fear in people was palpable. The tiny church was packed, people shoulder to shoulder on the pews. Barely anybody spoke, but they all wanted answers, reassurance, and for this, they turned to the small, portly man in a dog collar who stood before four hundred pairs of eyes opening and closing his mouth, unable to form any words.

'Perhaps ... perhaps, in this troubling time,' Reverend Owen said, 'we should begin with the Lord's Prayer.'

He bowed his head, but before he could utter 'Our Father,' one of the miners at the front stood and shouted, 'I'm not interested in my daily bread. I want to know what is going on.'

The man's name was Ellis. Merrick had been on shift with him a few times. He was a rabble-rouser, forever trying to cause dissent and strikes. Normally, people ignored him. Folk in Penyrhyll liked the quiet life, but nobody was ignoring him now.

A clamour erupted. People cried, 'Yes, tell us, tell us!' Some started shouting and jeering. Children cried and Merrick felt Emily's hand squeeze his.

Owen was out of his depth and knew it. He appealed to Maddox on the front row with his eyes, the most senior man there.

Maddox stood and turned to face the congregation, raising his hands requesting silence. It took some time, but eventually the clamour died down, the jeering stopped, and the church fell silent.

'I wish ...' Maddox began, his ruddy face strained, his nose billowing as he tried to form his words. 'I wish I had answers for you. The truth is nobody has any idea what has happened, not me, not Mr Llywelyn.'

'Then where is he?' Ellis shouted.

Maddox glared at him, his nostrils twitching. 'Back at the pit, waiting for help from the Coal Board. They're sending in a rescue team. Until then, all we can do is sit and wait and hope our comrades are returned to us.'

'My brother wasn't!' The voice belonged to Thomas

Davies. He stood at the back with his mother. It was the first time Merrick had laid eyes on her since Davies had vanished. She'd aged, becoming withered, grey, wasted. Slowly dying from a broken heart.

'Now listen to Mr Maddox,' Reese said, getting to his feet. 'There has to be a reasonable explanation for all this. Folk don't just vanish into thin air, not even down the pit.'

'Then where are they?' Ellis shouted.

Reese and Maddox looked at each other, both offering gentle shrugs.

'I wish I knew,' Maddox said. 'But the Coal Board will get to the bottom of it, I'm sure.'

'And what about our livelihoods?' Ellis shouted. 'What about our jobs?'

Merrick knew the answer to that. They were finished. Penyrhyll Colliery would close. You didn't lose over a dozen men and expect to stay open. Merrick suspected despite all the fears and apprehensions concerning Foweather and the others, this was what scared them all the most. Their lives were about to change. Dramatically.

'Let's just wait to see what the Coal Board says,'

Maddox said. 'I'm sure it will all come right in the end.'

Chapter 11

The investigation took a month. The National Coal Board called in experts from all over the country to try to uncover what happened to the missing men. Even a government minister came to the pit, as well as leading Union officials. Yet, strangely, Merrick never saw anything in the TV or newspapers about what had gone on, and nobody issued any statement and no answers were given.

The pit remained out of action. The large iron gates at the colliery entrance stayed closed, secured by a thick chain and heavy-duty padlock. The pit wheel didn't turn and the men survived on half pay, which fell to a quarter by the time the Coal Board left.

Nobody knew if the pit would ever reopen.

People were getting anxious, desperate. Fights broke out at the pub nearly every night. The shelves in the local shops were bare. Merrick rarely ventured out, and insisted Emily didn't too. She was showing now, her normally lithe figure bloated as she entered her third trimester. She said her lump made it hard for her to sleep, but Merrick doubted it was the pregnancy keeping her awake.

A week following the departure of the Coal Board, Merrick awoke early. Despite not having to get up for work, he continued to wake at 6.30, and no matter how hard he tried, he could never get back to sleep.

After checking the time on the alarm clock, he realized the bed beside him was empty. He swung his legs to the floor. His naked body puckering from the cold. They'd not had the heating on all month. Couldn't afford it. But ignoring the chill, he strutted downstairs, finding Emily staring out the winter.

'You okay?' he asked.

She turned round. She looked tired, large, dark shadows encircling her eyes.

'It's foggy,' she said.

Merrick shrugged.

'Don't normally get fog this time of year,' she said, turning back to the window.

He joined Emily at the window. It was light, the sun having risen an hour earlier, but Merrick couldn't see the street outside, just a white veil. Soupy thick.

'Must be a blanket of mist from the mountains. It's happened before. It'll lift by mid-morning. Do you want a cup of tea?'

She smiled thinly and nodded.

'Then go put your feet up. I'll bring it through.'

Merrick trotted off to fetch his dressing gown, hiding his modesty, before padding downstairs to the kitchen. It was even colder there, the tile floors like walking on ice. As he filled the kettle, he stared at the fog outside. It shrouded almost everything, except the Black Mountain, the ominous shape of which he could just make out, and when he squinted, he could see the outline of the pit wheel too.

He shuddered but did what he always did when thoughts of Foweather and Vaughn and all the other missing miners entered his mind, he pushed it back, concentrating on his wife and the new baby, worrying, without work, how on earth he was going to feed them.

Chapter 12

Merrick had been wrong. The fog didn't lift in the morning. It didn't lift all day. Even when night fell, the thick mist hung over the village turning the dark night as black as coal.

Merrick had stayed in all day, but come ten o'clock, a commotion sounded outside. Emily was sitting watching TV, the screen flickering with static and noise, and she sat up like a startled Prairie Dog. 'What's that?'

Merrick walked to the window, squinting, trying to peer through the soup. He caught a glimmer of lights and could hear voices, deep baritones.

'Wait here.' He threw on his luminous work jacket, grabbed the flashlight from the kitchen drawer and stepped outside.

The fog was as cold as it was thick, chilling Merrick's throat and lungs as he breathed it in. He could taste it too. It was like scorched air. And it was so thick he couldn't even see his own feet, which was why he found himself bumping into somebody on the pavement.

After cursing, Merrick realized he'd just clashed with old Dr Pryce, medical bag in one hand, flashlight in the other.

'Dr Pryce, so sorry ... I—'

'Is that you, Dylan?' another voice said out of the soup. Merrick recognized the deep tones.

'Mr Maddox, what's going on?' he asked, shining his flashlight onto Maddox's face as he fetched up beside the out of breath doctor. Both men looked alarmed and frightened.

'It's Llywelyn!' Maddox said, through breathless pants before he and the doctor barged past Merrick, scurrying down the cobbles as fast as the fog permitted, leaving Merrick motionless as they disappeared through the fog.

Only after several stunned seconds did he run after them, following the clip clop of their shoes as they headed to the colliery.

Minutes later, the vague silhouette of the pit wheel cut through the fog. Merrick didn't know how many people stood outside the gates to the colliery, but he could hear a clamour of voices and saw flashlights.

Maddox and the doctor pushed through the scum

to where Eric Barnes the constable stood before the gates, helmet and uniform on, doing his best to push back the curious crowd trying to peer through the fog.

When Barnes spotted Dr Pryce, he stepped aside , which was when Merrick saw Llywelyn.

At first, all he could make out was a shadow on the gates slipping in and out of the mist. Then as he stepped closer, the shadow took a familiar form. It was in the same pose as the crucifix adorning the church altar.

Llywelyn was in a Christ's pose. Arms outstretched. Wrists lashed to the gate. Head slumped to his clavicle. Yet it wasn't until Dr Pryce shone his flashlight at the mawkish figure, did Merrick see the true depravity.

Llywelyn's mouth had been stuffed with coal, forcing his cheeks out, but it was the sight of the stomach cut open, bowels and guts hanging from the belly like an umbilical cord dripping gore onto the cobbles that caused Merrick to throw up.

Chapter 13

Dr Pryce's surgery was small, a sitting room in a converted pit house. He'd been village GP for fifty years and was a kind and gentle old man, used to tending winter flu and bronchial problems. Not mutilated corpses.

Merrick and Maddox had helped PC Barnes carry the body back to the surgery. With the fog, Barnes doubted any police units would be able to get over the mountains until morning, and they couldn't just leave it where it was.

They had laid it down and Pryce covered the body in a white sheet, through which blood immediately seeped. He then opened his medical cabinet and pulled out a bottle of Brandy, pouring them all a drink.

'Who could have done it?' he said, wincing as the alcohol trickled down his throat.

'Take your pick,' Barnes said, removing his helmet and placing it under his arm as he drank the brandy. 'I've a list of suspects 200 strong.'

Barnes was old for a constable, close to fifty, but

he'd been the village's Bobby for as long as Merrick could remember. He doubted there was much opportunity for promotion in such a remote area but Barnes always seemed content, happy with this lot. Not today. His mouth followed the contours of his drooped moustache, furrows rutted his brow and he stared through narrow, grim eyes.

'I can't believe any of my members could do this,' Maddox said. He looked visibly shaken. Hands trembling as he scratched at his unshaven face, voice wavering as he spoke. His rock-like countenance had turned to blancmange.

'I know he wasn't popular,' Merrick said, looking at the bloodstained sheet. 'But this is … inhuman.'

'You wouldn't believe what people can do when tempers run hot,' Barnes said.

'Who found him?' Merrick asked, more out of curiosity than suspicion.

'Reese,' Maddox said.

'Jerome Reese?' Barnes asked.

Maddox rounded on him. 'If you think he could have had anything to do with this, you are mistaken.'

Remembering his position, Barnes put down the

glass of brandy and took his notebook from his top pocket, leafing through it to find a clean page. 'I'll need to speak to him, but do you know why he was there, out in this thick fog?'

Maddox got defensive, regaining some of his truculence, raising his voice. 'Checking the damned colliery gates, making sure people haven't tried to get in and make off with the copper and lead, a job you should have been doing. Spend too much time in the Prince of Wales, that's your problem, Eric.'

Barnes straightened, but even with his chest puffed out, he was still two hands shorter than Maddox. 'I'd watch your tone, Owen. I'm not one of your union members, remember? I'm just trying to find out the facts, that's all.'

'Mr Maddox is right,' Merrick said. 'Jerome Reese couldn't have done it. I've known him since we were at school. He ain't got it in him.'

'And who has, tell me that?' Pryce said. 'I was there to spank the backsides of nearly every one of you when you came from your mother's womb. I know every face in this village, and aye, there are some rotten apples, but I'd never have thought there was a single person in Penyrhyll capable of this.'

'Things have been a little ... strained of late,' Merrick said, realizing he'd not touched his drink. He knocked it back, swallowing the fiery alcohol in one mouthful.

'Things have been strained before,' Pryce said. 'This village survived two World Wars, depression, rationing. Nothing like this has happened before.'

'Where is Reese now?' Barnes asked.

Maddox shrugged. 'Probably back home, but I'd wait until morning if I were you, Eric. People are quite rightly upset. You don't want to go upsetting them anymore.'

'He's right,' Merrick said. 'Best wait until morning. I'll come with you. I know Jerome better than most.'

'I'll come too,' Maddox insisted. 'I don't want you bullying him into some sort of half-arsed confession.'

Barnes nodded. 'Okay. Early though. I want to speak to him before the constabulary gets a chance to send people over, which I'm sure they'll do as soon as the fog clears.'

Merrick looked out the surgery window and the thick fog blanketing the night.

'If it clears,' he said, quietly.

Chapter 14

The fog was just as thick come morning. Merrick figured in normal circumstances, a summer fog lasting two days would cause some consternation in the village, but the events of the previous night made thoughts of the weather irrelevant.

With their collars raised, breath steaming and adding to the fog, Merrick Maddox and PC Barnes headed to Jerome Reese's house.

It was identical to Merrick's home, and nearly every miner's house in the village. A two-up, two-down, basic construction terrace, with outside toilet and passageway cut through the bland brickwork, where the rubbish bags piled high next to Reese's push bike.

Mary answered the door wearing her nightdress, baby in her arms, its head buried beneath the fabric as it suckled at the partially exposed breast.

She looked tired, eyes like a mole, but they widened on sight of the three men stood at her front door.

'Mr Maddox, PC Barnes—what are you doing

here?' she asked, before smiling hello to Merrick.

'Sorry to intrude, Mrs Reese, but we need to have a word with Jerome,' Barnes said, bobbing on his heels. 'About last night.'

She nodded and widened the door, the babe in her arms unperturbed as the three men strode into the hallway.

'He's not taken it well, seeing Mr Llywelyn like that—not that he told me much. Haven't been able to get much of a word out of him. He's not slept, Mr Maddox. I'm worried he'll make himself ill.'

Maddox placed a friendly hand on her shoulder. 'Perhaps you could make some tea, Mary?'

She smiled thinly, prised the baby from her breast and slipped her bosom back in her nightdress before gesturing to the sitting room. She then made her way to the kitchen, patting the baby on her shoulder, silencing its demands for more milk.

They found Reese sitting in his underpants, a bottle of beer in his hand. Several empty ones on the side table beside his armchair. He was smoking a roll up, the ashtray on the arm of the chair overflowed with used butts.

He stood when Maddox and Merrick walked in. 'Mr Maddox, Dylan, what are you ...'

He tailed off as Barnes strode in and removed his helmet then nodded a meek hello.

'I'm guessing you know why we're here,' Barnes said, placing his helmet on a side table.

'About Mr Llywelyn, yes, but I told Mr Maddox everything last night.'

Merrick hadn't seen much of Reese since the pit closed. He hadn't seen much of anybody, but his old classmate looked weak, gaunt and pale.

The drink probably wasn't helping. With no work, many of the miners had taken to booze, and for a group of people unused to the regular hours of normal people, six in the morning wasn't unusual as it may have appeared to begin drinking. However, there seemed more to Reese's decline than just drink and depression. He looked as if his very life had been sucked out of him, leaving just a shell of flesh, skin and bone.

He'd had a shock, yes, but so had all of them, but Reese looked as if he had been going downhill for a long time. His hair had thinned, his nails were long and uncut, his fingers, stained with nicotine, trembled.

'I need you to go through it with me again, before CID arrives later,' Barnes said, glancing at the foggy morning outside the window. 'If they arrive.'

'Not ... not much to tell,' Reese said. 'I just went to check the gates, like Mr Maddox had asked ... and ... and that's when I saw him, strung up like that.'

He took a slurp of beer. The bottle trembled terribly as he put it to his lips and his eyes were wide, yellow not white, with veins like cobwebs crisscrossing them.

'Then what did you do?' Barnes asked.

'Ran to Mr Maddox's house then came back here,' Reese said. 'I was worried for my Mary and Cathy.'

'Understandable,' Maddox said.

'Why didn't you get me yourself?' Barnes asked. 'You know where I'd be, didn't you?'

The whole village knew where Barnes spent his evening, propping up at the bar of the Prince of Wales, but Reese just shrugged, but Merrick knew why. Maddox was the go-to man in the pit, and for many that meant he was the go-to man on the outside world too.

'Did you see anybody near the gates when you went to check them?' Barnes asked.

'Couldn't see anything in the fog,' Reese said. 'I just ran for it ... I wasn't hanging around, not with whoever had done that on the loose ...'

Mary walked in carrying a tea tray, silencing the room. Merrick doubted Reese had told her all the gory details. He himself had spared Emily the worst of it. Even so, hearing of Llywelyn's death shook her badly. She barely knew the man, but it didn't stop her sobbing uncontrollably for most of the night. She was scared, terrified even. It worried Merrick. He was concerned not just for her sanity, but also for the health of their unborn child.

Mary shared the same fearful look as Emily, withdrawn and diffident. Many of the women of the village looked like that now. The events of the last month or so had shaken them all, turning the normally garrulous and outspoken miner's wives familiar to all in Penyrhyll, into quiet, meek and fragile little women.

'Where's the baby?' Reese asked, as his wife set

down the tray.

'In her crib. Sleeping.'

Reese nodded.

'Perhaps you should try to get some sleep too,' Maddox said. 'You look exhausted, Mary.'

Mary shook her head. 'I'm all right, Mr Maddox, and who can sleep with all this going on?' She curled her lip and shook her head. 'It's the devil's work, Mr Maddox. I fear for us all, honestly I do.'

'Come on, Mary, let's not get hysterical about it,' Maddox said.

'Mr Maddox is right,' Barnes said. 'This is a crime, a brutal and heinous crime, but still just a crime none-the-less.'

'But ... with the disappearances ...'

Maddox grabbed her by the shoulders and shook her very gently. 'Now you listen here. You and Jerome need to be strong, for that young 'un upstairs. Do you hear?'

She proffered a weak smile before scurrying out with the empty tea tray while Reese returned to his beer.

Chapter 15

When Merrick returned home from seeing Reese, he found a visitor in his front room: Reverend Owen.

The ageing vicar, a saucer and teacup in one hand, stood and held out his hand on sight of Merrick. 'Dylan, how are you?'

'Fine,' he said, realizing his wife must have called the clergyman to talk things over.

It irked him.

Merrick knew Emily didn't share his lack of faith but he felt betrayed somehow, as if her need for Christian comfort somehow diminished him as a husband, but he smiled politely and sat beside his wife, who'd obviously been crying because her eyes were red and puffy.

'I was just telling Emily that the events of the last few weeks have been sent to test us, but as long as we stay strong and retain our faith, all will be well. Don't you agree, Dylan?' Owen smiled genially.

'Won't help Llywelyn much, will it?' Merrick replied.

Owen lowered his eyes. 'Such a tragedy, but we all

need to be strong in face of such ... trials.'

'It wasn't a trial, it was murder,' Merrick snapped.

'Dylan!' Emily glowered at him, a scowl replacing the teary eyes.

Merrick sighed. 'I'm sorry, Reverend, been a trying few days.'

'That's quite understandable,' he said, putting down his cup and saucer and getting to his feet. 'Perhaps you might think about coming to church this evening? I shall be holding a remembrance service for Mr Llywelyn.'

'We'll be there,' Emily said, lowering her eyes at her husband. 'Won't we? It's the least we can do for poor Mr Llywelyn.'

Merrick nodded. 'I'm sure we can make it, but I wouldn't expect a big turnout if I were you, Reverend. He wasn't a very liked man.'

Owen proffered a thin-lipped smile before picking up his hat he'd laid on the back of the chair. He plopped it on his head as he headed to the door. 'With any luck the fog will clear soon and the police will be able to get through.'

'With any luck,' Merrick repeated, escorting the

Reverend to the door.

In the hallway, an awkward silence fell between the two men. After a long second, Owen broke it with an anxious smile. 'I'll see you tonight then, Dylan?'

Merrick nodded.

Owen clapped Merrick on the shoulder. 'You will look after that wife of yours, won't you?'

Merrick forced an affirming smile, and then let the Reverend out into the fog.

Chapter 16

They never made it into church. At six o'clock, Merrick and Emily left the house, Merrick in shirt, tie and jacket beneath his overcoat, the same suit he wore on his wedding day and Emily in the only dress that still fitted her, her stomach ballooning through the green fabric.

The fog was still thick so they couldn't see anybody about but heard the clip clop of shoes on the cobbles and pavement, suggesting a few others were heading to church too.

And when Merrick and Emily made it to the cemetery gates outside the church, they saw the outline of dozens of other folk, suggesting half the village was congregating outside.

Slowly, the outlines became clearer, and it took a few seconds for Merrick to realize why. Then it dawned on him, the fog was lifting.

It was like the evaporation of steam from a kettle. One moment the air was thick with mist, a mist that chilled and shrouded all who stood before the church, the next it dissipated, almost instantly, as if some giant vacuum had sucked it all away, revealing the sun hanging in the west brightening the afternoon to almost a glare, the heat from it drenching and warming Merrick's face.

'I don't believe it,' he said, as the villagers around him all appeared from the lifting fog. He saw Maddox and Dr Pryce, Constable Barnes, and all their wives and children and a dozen other villagers besides. No sign of Reese or Mary, but that didn't surprise Merrick.

Everybody looked stunned by the sudden dispersal of fog, and then a few people gasped. Hands shot up to their mouths in disbelief and it wasn't until Merrick turned that he realized why.

Behind them, a line of men shambled up the street. They walked like lost little boys, shuffling their feet, heads glancing about left and right, eyes blinking wide with confusion as if they had just woken up. Black coal dust covered their faces, but Merrick recognized every single one of them: Foweather, Vaughn, Davies. All the missing men.

For a long moment, nobody spoke. Not the missing men. Not any of the villagers. Everybody stood in bewildered silence. Stunned. Shocked.

It wasn't until a voice croaked from behind the throng of villagers. A woman's voice, a meek and weakened voice, but a voice filled with ecstatic joy.

'Richard ... Richard!'

Mrs Davies ran to her son, stumbling and staggering on her ageing legs, positively falling on him, clutching him tight around the neck as she showered his blackened face with kisses.

Foweather's wife and children did the same, running up to their missing husband and father, and then all the villagers fell into an exuberant rapture of laughter and cheer, at the realization that the lost miners had been returned to them.

Chapter 17

They took all the missing miners into the church. Barnes, Dr Pryce and the Reverend went in with them. Everybody else was asked to stay outside, much to the chagrin of Maddox, who paced up and down, as did the families of the disappeared men who showed signs of both delight and frustration.

It was a long wait. Merrick, Emily clutching his hand tight, waited patiently with the others, where everybody kept their voices to murmured whispers and a few breathless prayers.

Eventually, the church door opened, and out stepped Dr Pryce with Reverend Owen close behind.

'What did they say?' Maddox demanded to know. 'Where have they been? What happened?'

Pryce shook his head, putting down his medical bag and arching his back before shaking his head. 'Nothing.'

'What do you mean nothing?' Maddox said, as the villagers gathered round, all asking the same question. 'Where have they been?'

'None of them seem to remember anything,' Pryce

said. 'Barnes is still interviewing them, but it seems they have no memories of the last month, where they've been, what happened to them. Nothing.'

'They must have been somewhere. What have they been living on?' somebody asked over Merrick's shoulder.

Pryce shook his head. 'No idea, but they are all in good health. As far as I can tell, none have suffered any injuries or physical trauma.'

A clamour erupted as people demanded to know more, but Reverend Owen silenced the crowd with a raise of the hands, like Moses as he parted the Red Sea. 'Perhaps, we should all just be thankful our loved ones have been returned to us. Maybe it would be appropriate if we all bowed our heads and thanked our Lord for this wonderful news.'

He closed his eyes and lowered his chin, clasping his hands together. Nobody else moved, not at first, but one by one, as Owen started giving thanks, the villagers brought their hands together and joined in the prayer, even Maddox, until the church door opened again and Barnes strutted out and the mumblings to God ceased and Owen had to fire off a quick, 'Amen.'

The constable was accosted by a dozen voices at once. Barnes had no answers for them, and as he fended off the clamour and told the villagers that they could join their loved ones if they wish, Emily squeezed Merrick's hand tighter, almost crushing his knuckles.

'Dylan, I want to go home,' she whispered. 'I don't like this.'

Merrick wanted to stay. He wanted to know what had happened, but he doubted with the throng of erstwhile widows and orphans now reunited with their loved ones, he could find anything out, so he nodded.

'Okay, but I'd like to call in on Mary and Reese, just to make sure they're okay.'

She smiled. 'Okay, I'd like to see Mary anyway.'

With a clench of their clasped hands, the pair slipped away and left the church.

Chapter 18

As Merrick and Emily travelled through the village, word began to spread about the return of the miners. People stopped them on the street, asking what was going on, others dashed down the cobbles to find out for themselves. So after banging on Reese's door and getting no answer, Merrick suspected Reese and Mary had gone to the church too and voiced as such to Emily.

'No, we'd have passed them,' Emily said, as Merrick rapped his knuckles against the door once more.

'Well, they ain't answering. Maybe they're having a lie down.' He nodded to the front window, where the curtains were drawn.

Emily didn't look convinced. She bit at her lip and crouched to look through the letterbox.

'Mary, it's me, Emily!' she part whispered, part shouted. She looked up, shaking her head. 'Maybe they are in the yard.'

'I'll go look, Merrick said, before sidling around the house to the passageway where he stepped over the bin bags and squeezed past Reese's bicycle.

The gate to the backyard was unlocked. So he creaked it open and ducked under the washing swinging lazily on the line.

'You here, Jerome?' he shouted, as he opened the back door.

Silence.

He stepped inside, noting the dirty plates piled around the sink and dirty laundry sitting in a basket before an empty washing machine. Merrick felt a trickle of trepidation. One thing he knew about Mary, she normally kept a clean home.

'Mary! Jerome! You at home?' he called, stepping from the kitchen to the hallway. He could see Emily's eyes staring through the letterbox. He nodded to the front room and knocked on it before pushing it open.

'Jerome, it's me—'

He spun round, turning his back on the sight that had just confronted him, a sight his brain refused to acknowledge.

Reese was hanging from a ligature strapped to the light fitting in the middle of the ceiling, but his old friend's hanged body hadn't forced his hand to his mouth, preventing the bile from spewing out. No, it was giving seeing Mary lying spread-eagled on the floor beneath her husband, a red cloth resting over her stomach, the child's face down on top of her breast sleeping serenely. Although Merrick knew the baby wasn't sleeping, and what covered Mary's belly was no cloth.

He raced to the front door, opening it to a startled Emily.

'What ... what's going on?'

He grabbed her by the shoulders, speaking sternly and firmly. 'Go home. Go straight home and lock the door. Don't open it for anybody other than me. I'll be back soon.'

'What's happened?' she demanded to know.

'Just do it!' he snapped.

She nodded obediently, turned and trotted quickly down the hill.

Once she was out of sight, Merrick sprinted back to the church to fetch Barnes.

Chapter 19

Merrick and Maddox were standing in the hall when Dr Pryce and PC Barnes came out of the sitting room like two spectres, pallid, faces gaunt, eyes sallow. Disbelief etched their brows and their voices shook.

'I cannot believe anybody, let alone young Jerome, could do such a thing,' Pryce said, breathing heavily.

Barnes held up a bloodied carving knife in his handkerchief. 'Poor lass didn't stand a chance.'

Merrick shook his head. 'I can't get my head round it. I know he was taking things badly, but ... this.'

'I blame myself,' Maddox said, clutching his forehead. 'I should have kept a closer eye on him. I could tell he was close to breaking, but I never imagined ...'

'Why would you?' Barnes said, taking out a polythene bag and dropping the murder weapon inside. 'At least it answers the question of what happened to Llywelyn.'

'But why Mary? Why the baby?' Merrick said. 'He was devoted to them, anyone could tell you that.'

'Depression does funny things,' Pryce said.

'I just don't believe it,' Merrick said. 'There has to be some other explanation to all of this.'

'Like what?' Barnes said, staring hard at him. 'Somebody else did it and framed him? C'mon, Dylan, I know you two go back a while, but it is clear. Reese had been tipped over the edge and turned into a monster.'

'He's right,' Maddox said. 'With everything that has gone on, it is not hard to believe something like this could happen. Perhaps we should take some solace in knowing it is all over. The men are back and I'm going to speak to the National Coal Board to see if they won't consider reopening the pit.'

'What do you mean, all over?' Merrick snapped. 'Nothing is over. We still don't know what happened. Where have all the men been? What happened to them? It's all too crazy for words. They'll never reopen the pit, not after this.' He waved his hand to the sitting room, where the shadow of Reese still hanging from the light fitting reflected off the glass panel on the door.

'They don't need to know about it,' Maddox said.

Merrick snapped his head towards him. 'You

what!'

Maddox looked at Barnes. 'Now that we know what happened to Llywelyn, who was responsible, maybe there is a case not to get anybody else involved.'

Barnes sucked air through his teeth. 'We're talking about a triple murder inquiry.'

'Yes, but one where the perpetrator has killed himself. Nothing left to investigate. If we kept a lid on it, I see no reason why the board won't reopen the pit, and then maybe this village can get back to some semblance of normality.'

'Normality,' snapped Merrick. 'Have you forgotten what's been happening this last month?'

'No, Mr Maddox is right,' Pryce said. 'This business has nearly ripped this village apart.'

Barnes looked down at the knife in the polythene bag. 'Perhaps I could have a word with the Superintendent, tell him it was all a false alarm.'

'I can't believe what I'm hearing,' Merrick said.

Maddox placed a hand on his shoulder. 'You've had a terrible shock, lad. Go home. Go look after that wife of yours. Leave us to handle all this.'

Merrick stared through wide, disbelieving eyes, shaking his head as he backed towards the front door but he said nothing. He just stepped outside and slammed the door shut before sprinting back to his house. He was clear in his mind. If they were not going to act, he would.

Chapter 20

'Em, it's me!' Merrick shouted as he dashed through the front door and snatched up the phone in the hallway. 'You are not going to believe what they want to do. They want to cover all this up.'

His fingers shook as he dialled. 'C'mon, c'mon,' he said, as the phone on the other end rang.

'South Wales Constabulary, how can I direct your call?'

'Hello, yes, I need to speak to someone dealing with the death in Penyrhyll. There's been another.'

'I beg your pardon,' said the voice on the other end. *'Who is this?'*

'My name is Dylan Merrick, I'm following up on the death in Penyrhyll that was reported earlier this week. Mr Llywelyn. Somebody was meant to be coming to investigate, but the roads have been all fogged up.'

'I think you might be mistaken. We've had no crime reports filed from Penyrhyll. Could you elaborate?'

Merrick fell silent for a moment then said, 'That's

impossible, Police Constable Barnes called it in.'

'*We've got no record of anything logged. Perhaps you should speak to the constable.*'

'I just have. He doesn't want you involved. Don't you see, they are trying to cover up the—'

He heard a click.

Merrick rapidly clicked the switchhooks on the top of the phone. 'Hello! Hello!'

The line had gone dead.

Paranoia rippled up his spine but something else replaced it. Alarm.

Emily hadn't answered him when he came in.

He slammed the phone down and shouted her name as he dashed into the sitting room and kitchen. Not finding her, he called again and cantered up the stairs, but the bathroom and bedroom and partially decorated nursery were all empty.

He glanced through the back window. Dusk encroached. He could see the ominous shadows of the pit wheel and Black Mountain but no sign of his wife. She wasn't in the yard, or in the passageway running behind the house where she'd taken to secretly smoking since falling pregnant.

His heart raced, threatening to burst through his ribs. He dashed round the house calling, shouting, swearing that she answer him. She wasn't there.

He ran into the street, head glancing left, right, hammering on neighbours' doors. Nobody answered. Curtains twitched and lights were switched off. The lively, community-centred street suddenly seemed empty, desolate. Lonely.

Merrick had no idea where Emily could be. Other than Mary, she had few friends in the village, and with the events of the last few weeks, Emily only left the house when the cupboards ran dry. Merrick glanced at his watch. The shops were closed.

He raced down the street, checking the passageways and alleyways, the waste ground behind the tenements, the children's play area, the bus stop. He even checked the pub, pulling open the door causing the few drinkers on their stools to spin round and the room to fall silent.

'What ails you, Dylan?' asked Bevin, the landlord, as he and the half dozen drinkers stared curiously at Merrick.

'It's my Em, anybody seen her?'

'She's not in here, lad,' Bevin said.

The drinkers turned back to their drinks, ignoring Merrick as his mouth opened and closed, words refusing to come out.

A month ago, an alarmed man running into the Prince of Wales looking for his wife would have resulted in curiosity, concern, offers for help. Now, all he got was indifference. Every villager seemed a stranger.

He searched as night fell, knocking on doors, nobody answering, running through the deserted streets. He barely saw a soul throughout his search, until it got close to midnight when he spotted a lonely figure ambling up the lane beneath the streetlights.

The skinny frame was familiar one.

Richard Davies.

The first missing miner.

Davies stopped on sight of Merrick, hailing him with a wave of the hand.

'Have you seen my Emily?' Merrick asked, panting.

Davies smiled. 'No, Dylan, I have not. I'm sure she'll turn up. I did.'

Merrick stepped back, a little disturbed by the

boy's tone. He looked down, noting Davies carried his mother's old wicker basket she used for collecting her groceries.

'Where you going at this hour?' he asked.

'Taking mother for a walk,' Davies replied, holding up the bag.

'Where is she—'

It was then Merrick noticed the trickle of red liquid dripping from the wicker basket. Davies smiled and opened the basket lid. The face of Mrs Davies stared up at Merrick, her mouth contorted in a permanent grimace, her severed neck glistening under the streetlight.

Merrick backed away, horrified. 'Jesus Christ! Oh, Jesus Christ!'

Davies laughed. 'He won't help you now. Nobody can help you now, Dylan.'

Merrick fled towards the only place he had left.

The church.

Chapter 21

Merrick saw a congregation of villagers outside the cemetery gates. They seemed to be holding some sort of vigil along the railings under the streetlights. They stood silent and still, about a dozen of them, men, women, children.

When he approached, Merrick realized it was no vigil, and the villagers weren't standing. They were suspended on the railings, bodies impaled by the spikes.

He stopped, gasping at the sight of mutilation. Some were gutted like fish, bowels dripping gore onto the cobbled pavement, others had faces and torsos flayed, bloody pulps strung up like legs of lamb in a butcher's shop. Unrecognizable.

He stood frozen, desperately wanting to tear his eyes from such depravity. He wanted to run, escape, but found his feet rooted to the spot, his eyes transfixed on the gruesome spectacle, scanning the monstrosities, hoping, praying, his wife wasn't among them.

And then one of the monsters moved.

A head lolled. A face rose up. Eyes opened.

'D...yla...n!'

It was a whisper of breath, not a voice, but Merrick recognized it, and despite the wretched creature only having one eye and just a hole where the nose had been, he recognized the torn police tunic matted with blood.

Barnes.

Merrick gasped, his eyes running along the arms to the railings running through the biceps like kebab skewers.

'I'll get help. Where's your radio? The phone lines are down.'

Barnes chuckled a hoarse whisper, the bloodied face grimacing. 'Join us ...Dylan ... Join us.'

The head flopped forward. Still.

Merrick wanted to fall to his knees and cry. The insanity of the situation was overwhelming. Tears streaked down his face. His heart seemed only to be beating once a minute. His breath was so rapid his chest heaved in convulsions, but one thought kept him on his feet. Emily.

He backed away, turned to run, but movement

caught his eye, figures shambling up the street towards the church.

'Dylan!' shouted one of the figures.

The deep baritone was strong, authoritative. It belonged to Maddox.

'Dylan, come join us! Come with us, Dylan. Come celebrate,' Maddox said, as he and the other figures stepped into the glow beneath the streetlight with the others. Foweather was there and Vaughn and Boyce and many of the other missing men, deranged grins on their faces.

'Yes, join us,' Davies said, swinging his gruesome shopping bag.

'You're one of us,' Maddox said, holding out his hands, as if offering peace. The palms were red with blood. 'So is Emily. Come, join your wife.'

Merrick felt as if Maddox had plucked his heart from his chest. His eyes were on the blood on Maddox's hands, his head scanning the mutilated corpses along the railings again.

'Where is she? What have you done to her?' he pleaded.

'Come, see for yourself,' Maddox said, smiling,

almost serenely, as if addled on drugs.

The men approached in a line, hands outstretched, blood covering their palms.

'Come join us.'

'Come to us, Dylan.'

'Come celebrate.'

Merrick backed away, slowly at first, but as they stepped closer, he turned and ran in the only direction left open to him, through the cemetery gates.

Weaving through the gravestones, stumbling, falling as he tried to get away, he stole a desperate glance behind.

Maddox and the others stood at the entrance, watching, staring. None stepped into the cemetery.

Merrick scrabbled to his feet and darted to the church, barging into the oak doors, flinging them open to a crash. He fell, hit the flagstones, scrambled to his feet, slammed the door shut and shot the bolts top and bottom, before collapsing and sliding down the door to the floor, where he sat and trembled and sobbed in the darkness of the church.

Several seconds passed before he heard another sound among the reverberations of his weeping. His sobbing was joined by a voice. A low voice. A deep voice. A man's voice.

Merrick got to his feet, fear trembling his hands and choking his breathing into short, rapid pants. He didn't speak. Dared not. He stood stock still, listening as the voice echoed around the church.

'... *they threw him into the pit, and shut it and sealed it over him, so that he might not deceive the nations any longer, until the thousand years were ended.*'

Merrick stepped from the alcove of the door. The church was dark, but a few candles had been lit near the altar. Here, he saw the outline of a lone figure kneeling and facing the crucifix hanging from the vaulted ceiling.

'*They had not worshiped the beast or its image and had not received its mark on their foreheads or their hands,*' continued the voice, as Merrick stepped slowly, quietly towards it. '*They came to life and reigned with Christ a thousand years.*'

As he fetched up beside him, Reverend Owen looked up from his beaten, leather-bound bible, the white of his dog collar glowing in the candlelight, his narrow eyes locked onto Merrick's before widening.

'Cast thee back!' he shouted, making a clumsy cross with his fingers as he shuffled backwards, falling prostrate. 'Get back, get back. You are a prophet of the beast!'

'Reverend, it's me. Dylan Merrick,' he said.

'In body, but falsehood is his weapon,' Owen spurted. He then started rambling, half praying, half pleading for mercy.

Merrick knelt, grabbed the man's shoulders and shook him violently. 'Reverend, I'm not one of them. Help me, they have Emily.'

Owen's breathing slowed from panicked bursts and his eyes softened. 'Dylan, I thank you, Lord. Dylan, my boy.' He threw his arms around Merrick, squeezing him. 'Thank you for sparing at least one from this madness.'

Merrick pushed him back, clutching his shoulders tight. 'Reverend, have you seen Emily?'

Owen shook his head.

Merrick shook him again. 'Do you know what's going on? What's happened?'

'We've gone and done it,' he said, fixing his stare at

Merrick. 'We've dug our way into hell and released the beast.'

'What are you talking about?'

'We've unleashed the great evil. It will consume everything, lay waste to everybody.' He pointed a gnarled finger at the door. 'Have you not seen the depravity outside that door? It started as soon as night fell. Those men we all thought lost. Well, they were lost, but not how we thought. As soon as dark fell, the killing started. They set upon their own families. Their own families, Dylan, their wives, their children.'

'What about Maddox? I've seen him with them. He wasn't one of the lost miners, why didn't they kill him?' Merrick asked.

He shrugged off Merrick's hands and gripped his own into fists, his eyes glistening in the candlelight. '*He* can seduce the weak-minded. We are powerless, Dylan. We are lost. Evil is upon us.'

His eyes suddenly narrowed and he stepped back, head tilting to one side.

He pointed his gnarled finger at Merrick. 'But you have been out there. Why haven't you been seduced by *him*?'

'Him? Do you mean Maddox?'

'Maddox is a servant. I mean *him*, the great demon. Satan himself.'

Merrick shook his head. 'I've never believed in the devil just as I've never believed in God. There has to be another explanation for this. Poison gas perhaps, sent everyone mad.'

'Are you such a fool you cannot believe what your own eyes are telling you?' Owen pointed outside again. 'People we know did that, Dylan. And they all died willingly. I stood and watched. I watched as they defiled our friends, our neighbours. I watched those being butchered rejoice in it.'

'What about you? Why didn't they attack you?'

'*He* dares not set foot in consecrated ground.' He shook his head. 'We are safe here. God will protect us, but out there, out there is *his* domain now.'

'I've got to find Emily,' Merrick said, turning to leave.

Owen grabbed him, clinging to his jacket coat. 'You cannot leave. If they cannot seduce you to *his* will, they will kill you, Dylan.'

'I can't stay, not while Emily is out there.'

Owen shook his head. 'If she is beyond those doors, she is lost, Dylan.'

'I don't believe that. I can't.'

Owen placed a palm on his shoulder. 'If she is alive, she is no longer of this earth.'

Merrick brushed off his hand. 'Not my Em, never!'

He strode to the door, but Owen leapt at his legs, rugby tackling him to the ground. 'I beg of you, don't go out there.'

'I have to find her!' Merrick shouted

He tried to force the old reverend from him, but for an old man, he was strong, his grip tight on Merrick's collar as he spoke, his mouth inches from Merrick's face.

'If you have to go, wait until daylight. The darkness belongs to *him*. Wait until morning. The warmth of God's sun will offer you some protection. Please, Dylan, trust me in this. You may doubt God's existence, but he doesn't doubt yours. Let him protect you, let him fight with you.'

Merrick wanted to shrug him off and race into the night, but filtering through the church, he could hear laughter from outside. It wasn't the laughter of celebration or men chuckling at a joke. It was menacing, evil. He could also hear his name being chanted, whispering into the church, echoing off the stone walls and stained glass. Then he heard the words, 'Emily is waiting for you.'

'Hear that?' Owen said. 'They're trying to entice you, Dylan, draw you out.' He pointed to the church door. 'If you go out there, you will be lost, Emily will be lost. Wait here with me, my boy. We'll go in the morning. We'll find your wife, with God's strength we will.'

Merrick couldn't take any more. He slumped onto one of the pews, hands over his face, tears drenching his palms.

He felt Owen's palm resting on his shoulder. The Reverend then gently moved Merrick's hands from his face, clutched them to his own and knelt.

'Pray with me, Dylan. Offer yourself to God. He will listen. Trust me.'

So for the first time in his life, Merrick fell to his knees and prayed.

Chapter 22

Merrick didn't sleep. Neither did Owen. The men just sat together silently, ignoring the taunts and chants from outside, Owen occasionally mumbling a prayer.

But as he had promised, when the first shafts of dawn's early light cut through the stained glass of the church, turning the gloomy vault into an array of reds and greens and yellows, the sounds outside silenced.

Merrick could feel the warmth of the sun shining through the windows. His despair, his fear, his anxiety over Emily seemed to lift, and he stood from the pew, strode casually to the church door and opened it.

The fresh valley air wafted into the church, further revitalizing Merrick. Outside it was bright, clear, warm. Everything looked normal. The birds whistled, the wind blew from the mountains and into the valley. The black mountain, that enormous mound of coal dust and slag, loomed over the village casting a shadow from the east. The pit wheel sat as it had always done.

For a moment, Merrick thought he'd dreamt it all and the hellish nightmare was over. All was as it should be, but Owen's trembling finger, quivering with fear, brought back the nightmarish realities as it pointed to the dismembered corpses strung up against the cemetery gates.

'By all that is holy,' Owen whispered.

There were more of them. At least another dozen bodies had been skewered to the iron railings. Bodies dismembered. Disfigured. Mutilated. A lake of blood glistened on the cobbles outside the church.

Ignoring the temptation to throw up, Merrick raced to the gruesome depravity, eyes scanning the hacked faces and flayed flesh, hoping his Emily was not among the dead that dripped their gore onto the cobbles.

'She's not here!' he cried triumphantly, after racing through blood and bowels and pieces of flesh and sinew on the ground. 'She must still be alive.'

Owen, keeping his distance from the wall of death outside his church, retained his somberness, nodding as his eyes scanned the grotesque figures. 'But for how long?'

'I have to find her,' Merrick insisted. 'Help me.'

'I ... I ...' Owen's eyes turned to the east and his

brows rose. He pointed.

Merrick followed the man's finger, seeing nothing other than familiar shape of the black mountain and pit wheel, and then he noticed something. The wheel was moving.

For over a month, the wheel that carried the men into the shafts below had remained still. Now, it turned. A whisper of grating metal wafted over the breeze as Merrick watched the wheel spin.

'Somebody's going down the pit,' he said.

'It must be them,' Owen said. 'Seeking sanctuary.'

'Emily might be with them.'

Owen pleaded to him with his eyes. 'Dylan, why not take this opportunity to escape, to flee this place? Save yourself.'

'I'm going nowhere without her. You said you'd help me.'

Owen shook his head. 'I'm an old man, what good am I? There are too many of them.'

'We have to try,' Merrick said. 'Besides,' he rested a hand on Owen's shoulder, 'we've got God on our side.'

Owen patted Merrick's hand and smiled.

Chapter 23

'What are we going to do?' Owen asked, as Merrick pushed open the colliery gates.

Like the church, they had been decorated with dismembered corpses, their gruesome death masks locked in a mixture of rapture and despair, mouths open, teeth exposed in a grotesque grin, limbs skewered onto the railings so they hung limp, heads down.

Merrick sighed with relief when he realized Emily wasn't among them.

'You are going back to get your old Anglia. Park outside the gates and keep the motor running,' he said to Owen.

'Where are you going?'

Merrick stared at the pit wheel, which no longer rotated, one of the empty elevators sat beneath the A-frame. 'I'm going down.'

'If you go alone, unarmed, they'll overpower you easy enough,' Owen insisted, his eyes unable to break the gaze of the bulging and bulbous death stares from his former congregation suspended on the gates. His mouth mumbled a prayer.

'Who said I'm going unarmed. Now, go get your car. If I'm not back up in an hour. Take off. Go get help.'

Owen protested, grabbing Merrick by the shoulder, but he shrugged off the old reverend and sprinted into the colliery.

He had his keys. They were always in his pocket. As he ran, he pulled them free, his fingers rifling through them, his sense of touch identifying each one. Front door key. The one for his locker. His moped key, which hadn't worked in over a year. And the long, iron key, heavier than all the rest put together. He slowed as he reached the equipment sheds and outbuildings dotting the rear of the colliery, finally stopping outside the concrete hut emblazoned with warning signs.

Keep Out, Danger of Death!

Authorized Personnel Only!

No Smoking!

Warning, Explosives!

He unlocked the heavy metal door and creaked it open. Inside was dark, so he turned on the light. The bulb, sealed and caged to prevent sparking, was weak, but it lit up enough for Merrick to see what he wanted.

A series of crates at the end of the shed contained what he wanted.

Dynamite.

They used it rarely in the mine. Modern plastic explosives were far more effective, and safer, but occasionally they still relied on Nobel's trusted sticks. And they would serve Merrick's purpose.

If Maddox and the others were down there, with Emily, and he was too late to save her, Merrick would blow the whole pit to kingdom come.

He used some duct tape to wrap three sticks together and repeated the process until he had two bundles of dynamite, which he stowed under his jacket, along with a coil of fuse wire. He checked his pocket for his lighter, and satisfied it was there, he dashed to the locker room, where he donned his helmet.

He then headed for the lamp room.

When he opened the door, he stopped short.

Conner sat behind his desk. Merrick could see the side of the man's flat, broad face. He was motionless, and at first, Merrick thought the man dead, but the lamp man's head turned slowly towards Merrick.

Merrick gasped as he saw two helmet lamps embedded in Conner's face where his eyes should have been. Blood trickled down his cheeks as the beams of light shone from his face.

'Where's ya token?' he rasped.

Merrick sidled past the desk, back to the wall. The two lamps set in Conner's face followed him as he scurried past.

'Where's ya token?'

Merrick ignored him, snatched a lamp and battery from the end of the desk and dashed to the pit wheel.

The elevator sat empty. Merrick pulled open the wrought iron gate and stepped inside, his heart thumping. After shutting the gate, he pulled the lever. Clanking and whirring sounded above his head as the great pit wheel creaked into life, and after a jolt, he descended.

He'd travelled in the pit elevator hundreds of times before, ranging from 300 hundred feet to 3,000 feet descents. None felt as long as this journey. With no other men in the elevator, he was alone with the sounds of clunking and clanging and creaking.

An age seemed to pass before the ascending lift flashed by. Merrick dashed to the grating and glanced up at it, checking if anybody rode it. It was empty.

Down he continued, the temperature rising with each second. Sweat trickled down his forehead. Every time he wiped it clear with his sleeve, more perspiration poured down his face. The air was heavy. The familiar stench of coal dust smelled alien, as if he were sixteen again, taking his first trip down the mine.

By the time the elevator jolted to stop, Merrick was drenched in his own sweat. After he pulled open the metal gate, the clanking metal almost deafening as it echoed down the mine, he stepped out.

After the reverberations from the elevator gate died down, the only sound Merrick could hear was his own laboured breaths. Ahead, he saw nothing but the seemingly endless tunnel that led to the new coalface and the rail lines for the mine train running down the middle. The lights flanking the walls were all on. The mine train wasn't there, so he'd have to walk, and with grim determination, he put his head down and marched briskly down the tunnel.

Chapter 24

Merrick heard the sounds long before he saw anybody. He was approaching the coalface. The machinery, mine train and boxes of equipment left abandoned when the pit closed blocked his view, but he could hear mumblings. Voices.

He scampered up to the mine train sitting at the end of the line, crouched, and half-crawled along it, poking his head above the carriages, glancing to see who was down there. Not until he reached the locomotive carriage at the end, did he finally see.

Several men stood around in a circle. They all had their backs to him, but he recognized them easily enough. Maddox was in the centre of them, flanked by Vaughn and Foweather. Merrick could also see Davies and Boyce and Bevin and about a dozen other men, some of whom had been among the missing miners, but none were speaking, the mumbling voice belonged to somebody else.

Merrick scurried from the train to a pile of crates behind the crowd of men. Peering over the top, he caught sight of Dr Pryce, his lips moving. Merrick listened intently, but he couldn't decipher the words. It sounded like gibberish. It was babble, as if the doctor spoke in tongues.

Then he heard a more decipherable voice. A voice that shouted 'No!' A voice he recognized instantly. A woman's voice. Emily's voice.

'Em!' he shouted, bolting from his hiding place.

He stopped, as everybody turned round, eyes widening on sight of him. None of the men wore helmet lamps, so they squinted as they stared at him, the same, blank, demonic expressions on their faces as he'd seen outside the church. Some had blood splattered on their clothes and faces, which also were smeared mixed with coal dust.

'Dylan, I knew you would come,' Maddox said, grinning. 'Come and join us.' He stepped aside, revealing Emily.

She lay on one of the generators, as if it were a table, naked barring the coal dust covering her bare breasts and distended belly. Her hands were trussed above her head, and her legs had been tied apart.

'Dylan, help me!' she screamed, squirming and arching her back, desperate to get free.

'What the hell are you doing to her?' Merrick shouted. 'Let her go.'

'I thought you'd be pleased,' Pryce said, something in his hand glinting. 'You are about to become a father.'

'They want our baby, Dylan,' Emily wept. 'They want to take it from me.'

Pryce held up a long, slender carving knife and dangled it above Emily's belly. '*Rege Satana!*' he shouted.

'Stop!' Merrick shouted, thrusting his hands into his jacket and pulling free one of the bundles of dynamite.

The knife wavered in Pryce's hand, as he caught sight of the bundle of explosives in Merrick's hand.

Merrick scrabbled in his pocket for the detonator wire, bit a piece from it and shoved it into the dynamite. He then pulled out his lighter, and flicked it, the flame flickering an inch from the wire. 'Anybody moves, and I'll blow us all to hell.'

'And kill your unborn?' Merrick said. 'Come, Dylan. Rejoice in his coming.'

'You untie her now,' Merrick said. 'Or so heaven

help me, I'll ...'

'Heaven cannot help you now,' Maddox said. 'Now put that away.' He turned and nodded to Pryce, who pulled back his arm ready to thrust it into Emily's belly.

'Don't!' Merrick lit the detonator wire.

It fizzed, the spark slowly making its way up the wire as it dangled from the dynamite.

'I told you, let her go.' Merrick estimated they had about thirty seconds.

Maddox's nostril billowed, his face stiffened, but he turned to Pryce and nodded. 'Untie her. We have time.'

Pryce cut through the duct tape holding Emily to the generator and she jumped free, sprinting to Merrick, the dynamite still burning in his hands.

'Where are you going to go?' Maddox asked, as Emily fell on Merrick, throwing her arms around his shoulder, sobbing. 'You know you cannot escape.'

'We'll see' Merrick said, his one arm cupping his wife behind her back, supporting her. With the other, he hurled the dynamite over the men's heads.

'Run!' Merrick shouted to Emily, as Maddox and

the others spun round, eyes watching the dynamite as it landed behind them.

'Stamp on the fuse!' Maddox shouted, as Foweather dashed to the dynamite fizzing on the ground, while Merrick bundled Emily into the mine train.

Merrick yanked the drive handle, and the train jolted backwards as Vaughn and Davies and Maddox sprinted towards them.

'Stop them!' Maddox shouted.

Blinding light flashed behind them, followed by a deafening roar and a pulse of energy that blasted Merrick and Emily flat into their seats while the train rocked.

Rumbling of collapsing rocks followed. Smoke and dust filled the tunnel, blocking the sight of Maddox and the others as the train hurtled along the track back towards the elevator.

A minute or more passed, before Emily spoke, trembling on his shoulder. 'Do you think they are dead?'

Merrick could barely hear her, his ears buzzed from the explosion. 'I don't know, and I don't care.

We're getting out of here.'

Merrick's heart raced as fast as the train sped back to the pit shaft, and only when he saw the empty elevator still waiting did it slow a little.

He stopped the train, and wrapping his jacket around Emily, helped her from the seat and into the metal cage.

'Don't worry,' he said as he shut the metal gate and yanked the starter handle. 'We'll soon be away from all this.'

The elevator jolted and slowly they ascended to the surface.

Chapter 25

Emily was barely conscious when they reached the top. Merrick propped her up with one arm as he opened the gate with the other. The cool afternoon breeze gusting down from the surrounding mountains awoke Emily a little.

'How you feeling?' he asked, helping her from the elevator.

'I'm okay, just feel exhausted—'

She screamed.

As Emily buried her head in his shoulder, Merrick turned to see a pair of feet dangling from one of the supports to the pit wheel. His eyes traced up the dead man's legs and stopped when they reached the dog collar around Owen's neck and the ligature fastening him to the steel of the pit wheel. His arms hung freely at his side. It looked to Merrick like the Owen's own doing, but then he saw, parked outside the colliery gates, the reverend's old Ford Anglia.

He reached up into the Owen's pockets and checked for the keys. When he didn't find them, he assumed, hoped, they would be in the car.

Keeping Emily's head buried in his shoulder, he led her through the lamp room, ignoring the repetitive chants for his token from Conner, the lamps embedded in his eye sockets still glowing. He kept her pressed tightly to him as he half-carried her out of the colliery, past the mutilated bodies adorning the gates.

When they reached the car, he saw the keys dangling in the ignition. After helping Emily into the front seat, Merrick looked back at the colliery, and then saw something that twisted an imaginary knife in his stomach.

The pit wheel was turning again.

He jumped into the front seat and turned the keys. The engine turned over but wouldn't fire.

'C'mon, c'mon,' he shrieked, eyes glancing at the turning pit wheel, his mind calculating how long it would be before the elevator appeared.

He kept trying the ignition. 'C'mon, c'mon, start damn you.'

'What's wrong with it?' Emily asked, her head lolling side to side, almost deliriously.

'I don't know.' He released the keys, knowing if he continued to try the battery would soon be dead. 'Wait here a minute.'

He flipped the catch and raced to the front of the car, peering into the engine compartment. His eyes followed the wires and cables. When his gaze reached the distributor cap and he saw the missing high-tension lead, he realized not only that the car wouldn't start, but also knew what Owen had used to hang himself.

He slammed the bonnet shut, unsure of what to do next just as the light began to fade and a cold chill enveloped him. His eyes shot skyward. Thick dark clouds blew across the sky, blocking the sun. A rumble of thunder sounded in the distance, and then rain speckled his face.

He dashed to Emily's door and yanked it open. 'We've got to go.'

Her head flopped towards him. 'But I'm too tired, Dylan. I can't.'

'You can and you will.' He dragged her from the car and hauled her down the street, the rain whipping at his face.

'Dylan, there is nowhere to go.'

He ignored her pleas, and with his arm supporting

her, he pulled her down the lane, unsure where he was going, but knowing he had to get as far from the village as possible.

It took nearly half an hour before they reached the outskirts of the village where she finally collapsed under the shadow of the black mountain.

'I can't go on,' she said, weakly.

'We have to carry on,' he insisted, but he could see how weak and frail she looked. Her skin was pale and her near naked body shook from the cold.

He lifted her up and squeezed her a little, trying to get some warmth into her, which was when he noticed something in the distance.

The pit wheel had stopped turning. Whoever was coming up in the elevator had arrived.

'God, please help us!' he mumbled, his eyes fixed to heaven.

The sky had darkened, becoming almost as black as the giant slagheap above his head. Merrick knew all was lost, but then he looked skyward again. Not a heaven. He knew God had abandoned them. But he stared up at the black mountain. That precarious pile of dust and soot and detritus from the mine.

He scrabbled around under his jacket, pulling free the remaining bundle of dynamite. He stuck in the remaining fuse wire and lit it, casting it at the base of the slagheap, before grabbing Emily by the arms and dragging her as far as he could while she screamed and writhed and shouted and bawled in pain.

They made it about fifteen yards when the dynamite exploded.

At first, Merrick thought he had misplaced his throw because after the loud roar and the eruption of smoke and soot cleared, the black mountain looked unmoved.

Yet, as he continued to haul Emily away from the shadow of the slagheap, a gentle rumble sounded. Along the flank of the slagheap, bits of coal and dust trickled down like a gentle stream. The rumbling increased. The trickles turned to streams then to rivers, and finally, with a reverberating roar the entire mountain of coal dust seemed to shift. Dust billowed up in plumes, swirling and choking Merrick, who dived on top of his wife, his lips mumbling prayers as the slagheap collapsed.

Chapter 26

Merrick emerged from the layer of dust like a survivor from Pompeii. Black from head to toe, choking dust in his mouth. He coughed uncontrollably trying to expel it and eventually puked up a thick sludge, clearing his chest.

All around him was dark, dust thick in the air, impenetrable, choking. He couldn't see, but plunged his hands into the shallow of dust and dirt feeling for Emily, pulling her limp body free.

He laid her on top of the slag, thrusting his fingers into her mouth to clear her airways, giving her the kiss of life.

For a minute, his heart refused to beat not until she coughed back into life, wheezing and gasping. He then carried her across the slag as far as he could manage, finally slumping onto the base of one of the hills that overlooked the village, where he gulped up the fresh air, which helped expel the remaining coal dust from his lungs.

It was then he surveyed the village. It was nearly all gone. Despite them both being covered and caked in coal dust, the slagheap had collapsed away from him and Emily towards the village. A million tons of coal and slag had washed over everything. The village was below a sea of black, thick dust, perhaps twenty feet deep in places. Even the colliery was covered, except for the pit wheel the top of which protruded from the filth.

Penyrhyll was gone, and so were its inhabitants, barring two lonely survivors, covered head to toe in coal dust, coughing and spluttering on the hillside.

Epilogue

Merrick paced up and down outside the delivery suite at Cardiff's University Hospital. It was a modern, state-of-the-art building, warm, air-conditioned, carpeted and a world away from the rural clinic where they had expected her to give birth.

They had wanted to get as far from Penyrhyll as possible. Merrick's sister had provided them with a spare room, and had also volunteered to be with Emily as she gave birth. The midwife had asked Merrick if he wanted to be at her bedside, but he declined. He knew many men did it nowadays, some even cut the umbilical cord, but he was old-fashioned when it came to things like that. His place was here, waiting patiently for his son, or daughter, to come into the world. Besides, he'd seen enough pain and suffering to last a lifetime.

Neither of them talked about Penyrhyll, not since the two men from the Coal Board visited when they first arrived in Cardiff. At least they said they were from the Coal Board yet neither had much of a clue about mining.

They questioned them for hours about the events of Penyrhyll. Merrick had told the truth. Left nothing out. He doubted they believed a word he said because after confessing to collapsing the slagheap, which had buried the town and killed God only knew how many of the remaining villagers, they didn't call the police. In fact, after they had relayed their story and the men left, he heard nothing about Penyrhyll. It wasn't even mentioned in the news. It was as if none of it had happened. As if the village had never existed.

Merrick didn't care. All that mattered now was Emily and their child. He'd have to find work, of course, and he had few skills outside being a miner, but he'd worry about that later. For the moment, as screams echoed out of the delivery room, he had more pressing things on his mind.

It was another five minutes of shouts and oaths and painful screams before his sister finally emerged, a broad grin on her face.

'Dylan, you're a daddy,' she said, sweat trickling down her forehead.

'What is it, a boy or a girl?' he asked, excitedly.

'Come see for yourself,' she said, widening the

door.

Merrick rushed into the delivery room where Emily lay in bed, a small bundle wrapped up in a blanket on her breast, a midwife and two nurses standing around smiling.

Emily, tears streaking down her cheeks, turned to Merrick and showed him the small, perfectly formed features of the baby's face. 'It's a boy, Dylan. We have a son.'

As the little face stared up at him, warmth flushed over Merrick's body. He felt his heart flutter like a butterfly drying its wings and his legs almost buckled.

'He's beautiful,' he croaked, perching on the edge of Emily's bed and sliding an arm around her shoulder. He looked up at the midwife. 'He is okay, isn't he?'

The midwife smiled. 'He's perfect. Ten fingers, ten toes.'

'What are we going to call him?' Emily asked.

'Maybe Bron, after your dad.' Merrick regretted saying it as soon as the words left his mouth. Her father had died when she was young but even uttering his name would have brought back memories of

Penyrhyll, breaking their unwritten taboo about bringing up the village.

'We'll talk about it later,' she said. 'There's no rush.'

Just then, the baby became animated, crying and pushing his tiny arms from the blanket.

'I think he wants feeding,' the midwife said. 'Do you need help?'

Emily shook her head and removed her breast from her gown. 'No, I suppose I'll have to get used to doing it on my own.'

The baby took to the teat like a drunk to a bottle, causing the midwife to smile. 'Hungry little fellow, isn't he? You must be pleased as punch, dad.'

Merrick didn't answer, he was too busy looking at the small mark on the baby's right hand as it clutched at Emily's breast. He pointed at it. 'What's that?'

The midwife peered over. 'Oh, that's just a little birthmark. Nothing to worry about. It's a queer shape, though. It almost looks like numbers. 999.' She chuckled. 'Maybe he'll grow up to be a policeman.'

Merrick staggered off the bed, knocking over a jug of water on the side table.

'Careful,' said the midwife. 'Are you okay, Mr Merrick? Do you need to sit down?'

Merrick didn't answer. His eyes were transfixed on the tiny hand clawing at his wife's breast. The birthmark didn't look like the emergency telephone code to him. He was looking at it from the opposite angle, where the three nines looked like three sixes.

The End

By the Same Author

MEGALANIA
Vile Beasts Series

Research scientist Suzanna Howard has reached one of the most unexplored regions on Earth, only to find a mining corporation has beaten her to it.

But more than gold has been unearthed in the interior of Papua New Guinea.

Animals thought extinct for over 10,000 years have been living undisturbed.

Until now.

When the creatures attack the intruders in their domain, Suzanna Howard finds herself allied to the very people she despises. As she battles to protect a species once thought extinct, she soon realizes the Megalania are not the ones on the endangered list.

SUCKERS
Vile Beasts Series

Whales are dying on the Scottish coast and cetologist Sarah Bennett wants to know why.

Something is attacking and killing these mighty leviathans.

Something voracious.

The source of the dead whales seems to be the sleepy fishing isle of Mol Mar, where police sergeant Maurice Bradley is investigating several bizarre killings, the victims left drained of blood.

With Sarah's help, Bradley discovers the deaths of the islanders and the whales are inextricably linked, and the pair soon find themselves battling a terrifying blood sucking menace from the sea, intent on devouring the island's inhabitants.

The White
Vile Beasts Series

Three soldiers maimed and traumatized in combat are intent on making it to the top of the world.

Lieutenant Jon Fowler and his team are not alone at the North Pole. A group of scientists are conducting research into climate change, while adventurers and tourists have arrived at a Russian Ice Station to sample the polar experience.

All are unaware that one of nature's most formidable beasts is roaming the ice sheets, a man-eater, hungry and desperate.

Fighting bad weather, Fowler and his team find they have to overcome more than their own adversities to save those stranded, alone and hunted in ... The White.

Sandflies
Vile Beasts Series

Dwayne Leary is a salvager, part of a team sent to strip an old oil refinery in one of the most inhospitable places on earth. But there is more than camels and nomads roaming the desert.

Besieged by insurgents, Leary and his crew realize their enemy is not on the outside.

Something else has infiltrated the oil refinery.

Something leaving Leary and the others paranoid, unsure of who to trust.

Something carried by ... The Sandflies.

Brock
Vile Beasts Series

Recently widowed Charlie May heads across the Atlantic with his two children, back to his former home, the sleepy English village of Hunters Heath.

Charlie encounters more than old flames and former rivals in the tranquil village.

The normally benign and timid wildlife have changed, turning into ferocious predators.

As the animals go on the rampage, attacking everyone on sight, the village falls under siege. Cut off and helpless, Charlie, with the help of his former girlfriend, tries to figure out why the normally docile animals have turned into such vicious killers, while battling to keep his two children safe from ... The Brock

ROGUES

They say elephants never forget...

Mercenary Frank Humbolt takes on one last job: to capture a rebel leader deep in the heart of Africa. Only he hasn't anticipated the local wildlife.

A group of rogue elephants, seemingly angered by years of poaching, are wreaking revenge and bringing wanton destruction to the region. Humbolt and his team soon find themselves hunted by both men and beasts.

To get out alive, Humbolt has to rely on a young zoologist for help, while the fate of an entire nation hinges on his very survival.

Dirty Deeds

Waynfleet International specialize in those dirty deeds that governments don't like doing themselves. However, things are not going well for Lt Col Harry Delaney and his band of mercenaries. A botched job in Albania and mounting debts has forced them to take their riskiest assignment yet: to replace the ailing president of the former Soviet Republic of Azjikistan with his exiled daughter.

The journey to Azjikistan takes Delaney and his motley crew from the streets of London, to Paris, Moscow, Las Vegas and Switzerland. En route, they encounter Russian agents, Islamist assassins, interfering spies, murderous thugs, a femme fatale, the Trans Siberian Express, and a despotic tyrant.

Intrigue and murder follow Delaney and his team every step of the way, but with so much at stake, this is one job they cannot afford to mess up.

Murder Laid Bare

A Hope and Carver Mystery

When a body is discovered on a nudist beach, the struggling seaside resort of Milhaven is thrust into the media spotlight. Fortunately, Inspector Hope has just arrived at the sleepy coastal town, much to the annoyance of brassy Detective Sergeant Elaine Carver.

Forced to work together, the temperamental Carver and rather prudish Hope delve into the dead man's past and uncover a darker side to the goings on at the seemingly innocent nudist resort.

Both Hope and Carver are themselves hiding dark secrets and have far more in common than they think. The investigation soon leads them on a path of self-discovery where they have to face their inner demons as they uncover the seedier side to middle class suburbia.

Death of an Angel

A Hope and Carver Mystery

When Milhaven's annual biker event culminates in a shooting, Hope and Carver are called to investigate. But with Carver struggling to juggle work with her personal life, and the pair facing nothing but a wall of silence, even she doubts that they can get a result this time.

As the collateral damage from the shooting escalates, and biker gangs clash in the once peaceful seaside resort, a taskforce prepares to take over the investigation, leaving Hope and Carver under pressure to find the culprit. But even if they can solve the case, Carver realizes it could all be too late for Milhaven, as the seaside town may never be the same again.

The Anderson Files

Inspector Anderson Omnibus

THE EYNHALLOW ENMITY
THE LOCH
PARADISE WOODS

Special Branch's most ill-tempered detective finds himself battling paranormal killers, loch monsters, psychopathic farmers, escaped apes and a zombie-ridden village in this collection of three, full-length novels.

Khan

When a young girl is found brutally murdered in London's Clapham Common, determined Metropolitan Police DCI, Elizabeth Grainger, finds herself thrust into an investigation that spans two continents.

While attempting to track down the vicious killer, Grainger struggles to cope with her disordered home life, and things soon get even more complicated when Khan, a tough, Delhi police inspector, arrives to assist in the investigation.

Khan's indomitable methods prove too much for Grainger, and as the case spirals out of control, she begins to wonder if there is more to the enigmatic Sikh than meets the eye.

About The Author

Robert Forrester is a writer and journalist based in Birmingham, United Kingdom. He is the author of the Inspector Anderson Mysteries, Hope and Carver Mysteries, the thriller Rogues, and the Vile Beasts Series

Printed in Great Britain
by Amazon